not so much appreciated

WARTS & CLAWS INC. SERIES
BOOK 5

CLIO EVANS

Copyright © 2022 Clio Evans

Cover illustrated by @poppypari (instagram)

All rights reserved. No part of this book may be reproduced or used in any manner without the prior written permission of the copyright owner, except for the use of brief quotations in a book review.

"An office is for not dying. An office is a place to live life to the fullest, to the max, to... an office is a place where dreams come true." — Michael Scott, The Office

warning!

HR Department:

Dear Reader,
There have been **R**eports of the following in this office: an **arachnid** monster, light Daddy kink, spitting, spanking, BDSM, Dom/sub dynamics, switch dynamics, web bondage, 'good girl', dirty talk via company phone, omega heats, knife play, mating bites, voyeurism, degradation, and more.

If any of this makes you uncomfortable, please report it to your HR rep immediately.

Not So Much Appreciated—
Warts & Claws Horn-y Resources

CHAPTER ONE
monday meetings

ALEX

It was Monday, and I was already regretting walking into the office this morning.

My head ached, but I ignored it as I sat at my desk. There were stacks of paper everywhere, coffee cups filling every empty spot on the desk. It was exactly how I'd left it on Friday when I'd gone home late.

This company was falling apart. Inferna had been a huge help, and we were working on fixing things, but I'd let it get too messy. Not to mention all of the terrible things that had happened.

I'd been living with the guilt. I didn't like it. I didn't like feeling responsible for what Alfred had done to my employees. I didn't like feeling responsible for everything that had happened to the omegas.

In the beginning, I hadn't known that I would cause so much pain.

Alfred was on my mind this morning. I hated him, hated everything he had done. I hated myself too.

I had made a lot of mistakes, and it was proving to be difficult to mend them. I was trying, but it didn't help that the wolf had been nipping at my heels.

The moment we had 'merged' the companies together was the moment things started to change.

It had started with Inferna, Art, and Calen. Because of them, I was set free after being imprisoned. That's when I realized the monster I had believed would never hurt me had done just that.

I had seen the terrible things he was doing when I wasn't passed out.

Then it had been Cinder, Mich, and Lora.

A couple of the other employees around here had been caught working for Alfred too. I had foolishly believed that maybe he would let me go, to let us all go.

I should have known better.

In all the time I had known him, he had never been one to simply quit.

Then there had been Billy, Jaehan, and Charlie. They had been lucky. I had been able to use Jaehan's magic to help us all, and for once, I had found myself feeling a little better about things.

I had helped. Kind of.

Ember, Minni, and Lea had been next. Ember's magic was strong, and I had known that for some time.

If I had acted before all of this, then maybe no one would have been hurt. That's what haunted me.

That's what made me want to stop showing up on Mondays.

But I couldn't quit. I wasn't a quitter. I had to keep going and fix what I had broken.

A soft knock came at the door, and I looked up, not surprised to see Anne.

Her skin was golden and dusted with scales, the snakes that surrounded her head swept up into a bun. She had the lower half of a serpent, her tail stretching out behind her.

She was stunning.

She also worked for me.

I didn't like that she was alone. I didn't want her alone with me. Every time I saw her, I could feel my chest clench, which was a red flag.

"Good morning," she said, giving me a bright smile. "I have the agenda for today ready for you. You have a lot of meetings. I know you just walked in, but I wanted to bring you a cup of coffee and talk you through it."

I didn't want her alone with me, and yet I'd somehow allowed her to become the first person that greeted me every morning.

The last couple of nights, I had dreamed about her too. I had woken up hard, my muscles tense and my body aching. I could barely remember what I had dreamed, but it had been very inappropriate.

"Sure," I said, nodding.

For such a powerful witch, I was weak.

Anne nodded and came into the office, bringing the cup of coffee with her. She handed it to me, her fingers brushing over mine as I took it.

Fuck, this was inappropriate. I bit back a groan and gave her a bland smile, sitting down in my chair with a sigh.

Anne went over to a table that was against the wall and started the coffee pot. I watched as she measured out the coffee grounds, her skirt hugging her ass in a way that should have been against HR guidelines. But our HR department was currently gone since they had all been working for a monster who wanted to use omega witches for their magic.

Well, there was Cinder, but the dress code was the least of our concerns.

It was my problem anyway.

Fuck.

I took a sip of my coffee, swallowing hard as she turned and came over to the desk. She started grabbing my empty cups, and I winced.

"You don't need to do that," I said, only slightly humiliated.

"I know," she quipped, raising a brow. Her soft lips pulled into a smile. "Just drink your coffee, boss. I know you were here late Friday working and that you're stressed. And you have at least five meetings today."

"Fuck. Five?" I hissed.

"Yep," she said cheerfully. "Some of it has to do with new hire interviews. Sylvia...she applied to work here, and Inferna approved her. So now she just has to be interviewed by you."

I frowned. "Inferna should have waited to interview her with me."

"Inferna is out today," Anne said. "And you were busy Friday. I can sit in on the interview with you if you'd like."

I nodded. "That should work. Thank you. Is Inferna okay? How in the hell do you know more about this office than me?"

Anne snorted, carting all the cups over to a table with a bin on top. "Well, first, I work on the same floor as everyone else. And second, I'm the secretary. I sit at the front desk. Everyone tells me everything, and I see what happens. Including how the shifting room is sometimes used."

I raised a brow but didn't say anything. I *did* know what happened in the office in that context and didn't care.

"Plus, she texted me this morning. Oh, and Art and Calen came in alone, both looking mildly frazzled without her."

I fought a snort.

The three of them complimented each other— and that made me want to throw up. I was happy about all of the matings that had happened in the office, but I was also jealous.

Did I want that?

Yes.

But I would never get that.

I had been around for a long time and had never met anyone who was my mate. I would know, too.

The idea of going into heat right now sounded like a nightmare anyway.

"So, the first meeting is an interview?" I asked, my eyes never leaving her.

"Yes," she said, coming back to my desk and taking a seat in the chair across from me. "Second and third are meetings with some of the team leads. Art is here today, so he'll be here for that, as well as Cinder."

I nodded, reaching for one of my sticky note pads and a pen. I scrawled down what she was saying, pausing to listen to what was next.

"Fourth meeting is with what is left of the corporate side of the company?"

Fuck. That was complicated. They weren't entirely aware of what was happening here, and I wanted to keep it that way. They did know that Alfred was.... *'not doing well'*.

What I wanted to say in my many emails to them was that the fucker was dead, but that was hardly professional.

"Fuck," I sighed. "That'll be interesting. I mean, it's my company."

"It is," Anne said, shrugging. "It'll be fine. And the last meeting is payroll. You and me."

"Oh," I said, writing that down. "What's with payroll?"

"Raises," Anne said.

"Ah," I said, chuckling. "Yes. It's the least we can do."

"Oh, and tomorrow, you have a meeting with the company that wants to have us work on a project with them."

"Okay," I said, leaning back in my chair. I looked up at the ceiling for a moment and then nodded. "Busy week already."

Anne nodded. "It is."

I looked at her directly and tilted my head, studying her. We stared at each other for a few moments, a light blush creeping into her cheeks.

"What else?" I whispered.

I didn't mean to sound like *that*.

There was a stretch of silence between us. One that made my heart beat a little louder.

She was a monster. Did that mean she could hear it beating faster?

Fuck.

She parted her lips, her diamond pupils expanding. "Well..."

My heart skipped a beat. I felt like the world had stopped, everything hanging on her words.

Her lips spread into a smile, and she looked away, breaking the moment. "Well, we get to work."

I stared at her for a moment longer and then nodded, forcing a smile. Forcing myself not to dig deeper, to not ask her if that's really what was on her mind.

"Okay," I said. "I'll see you when Sylvia gets here?"

"Yes," Anne said, rising from her seat. "Let me know if you need anything. And make sure to eat a granola bar at least, so your stomach doesn't growl in the interview."

"That only happened once," I said, but I was already reaching for the snack drawer in my desk as she headed for the door.

She waved and then grabbed the bin of coffee cups, leaving me alone to think about how all I wanted to do the rest of the day was bend her over my desk and fuck her.

CHAPTER TWO
interview

ANNE

I left Alex's office, thankful that he was a witch and not a monster like me who could hear hearts beating.

I dumped the bin of coffee cups in the kitchen, washed them quickly, and then went back to my desk right as the clock struck 9 a.m.

There were some monsters and witches already in the office, the chatter already beginning as they got settled at their desks. I went through the motions of saying hi and smiling. All the while, my thoughts were pinned on Alex.

He flustered me. No one flustered me. But there was something about him, even though I didn't necessarily trust him.

I saw a different side to him than everyone else did. The side that wasn't stoic, that wasn't the *Boss*. Every morning he came in looking like a whipped puppy, one that was trying to navigate a disaster he had helped create.

I didn't pity him necessarily, but I didn't like it.

What I did like was the way his bright blue eyes lit up when he saw me. Maybe it was just the coffee, but I'd started to look forward to seeing him every morning.

"Morning, Anne," Billy said, waving as he walked into the office.

"Morning," I said, smiling.

Jaehan and Charlie were behind him, the two of them talking to each other about their weekend. I watched the three of them with a smile.

They were sweet together. I was happy for them. Hell, I was happy for all the relationships that had happened in this office. Even with all the terrible events that had occurred, monsters and witches were still finding their happy endings.

I had grown up believing monsters didn't get happy endings. It had taken a long time to realize that didn't have to be true, that monsters could find love. With a human, another monster, or a witch.

"Morning."

I looked up as Art came over to my desk, leaning against the top.

"You look frazzled," I said.

Art made a face. "It feels weird without Inferna here, but I'm glad she's taking off. She's having a 'her' day, and that makes me happy."

I realized he was looking across the office and followed his line of sight, not surprised that it was on Calen. I smiled to myself. "I have an interview with Alex soon, and then you have some meetings today too."

"Oh, I know," Art said, shrugging. "I already checked my emails, Anne. I *do* work."

"I was just checking," I hissed playfully. "Goodness. You witches are so grumpy."

Art scoffed. "Don't compare me to Alex."

"I didn't compare you to anyone," I said, rolling my eyes.

"Here's the office," a voice chimed.

I looked up, not surprised to see Ember leading Sylvia in. Those two had become friends since they had been trapped together a few weeks ago.

It had been almost six weeks since Alfred had been officially banished. We'd all had time off for the holidays and even New Year's day. We were halfway through January, and everything had started to feel normal.

A lot of the omegas we had hired had finally settled in too. The monsters had calmed down, and for the most part — everything was harmonious. There were tiny little office wars that sprung up here and there, but it wasn't anything too bad.

Well, except for when one of the monsters clogged and flooded the restroom, which resulted in one of the witches slipping, which resulted in an almost war.

But aside from those little things, it had been good.

Sylvia had taken some time to herself after she'd gotten back into the world. I didn't know her too well, although I wanted to. Every time I saw her, I felt my stomach flutter.

Perks of being a bisexual gorgon who worked in the office— you could crush on your new hire and your boss too.

Sylvia had very pale skin, long silky black hair, and was wearing a dress that dipped down to her breasts. There was a red tattoo on her chest, reminding me of a black widow. She had four arms and then black spider legs that branched out of her spine. Her six eyes swept up to meet my gaze, holding it.

Fuck. I felt my stomach flutter. It wasn't fair that I was going to be in a room with these two, but I had to play it cool. I had to be a professional.

"Hi Anne," Sylvia said, giving me a slow smile.

She'd put on crimson lipstick too.

Professional.

Fuck me.

"Hi Sylvia," I said, smiling. "Alex is ready for us. I'll be joining in on your interview."

I could feel Art watching me with a raised brow as I rose from my chair, knocking over one of the pen holders. "Oops," I hissed, flustered now.

Art gave a very soft chuckle. "Have fun in your interview, Sylvia."

I would have hissed at him if he weren't my boss. Hell, I might have even let one of my snakes loose to bite him, but then Inferna would have to talk to me about violence in the workplace again.

Not that I was violent. It's just that witches were annoying sometimes.

The thought of Alex invaded my mind again, and I damn near hit my head on my desk as I reached down.

I grabbed the pens quickly, fixed them in their cup, and then grabbed the new hire interview sheet, moving past her and Ember.

"Come on," I said to Sylvia.

Ember reached out and gave one of Sylvia's hands a reassuring squeeze. "Good luck! You'll be on my team in no time."

"Thank you," Sylvia said, smiling again.

Fuck, she was too sweet.

My heart beat a little bit faster as I moved back out into the hall, my tail dragging behind me as I led Sylvia to the elevator. I hit the button to go to the next floor, turning to give her a reassuring look. Sylvia's eyes watched me, sending a chill up my spine.

The elevator doors slid open, and the two of us stepped inside. I pulled my tail in right as they shut, tapping the floor ten button.

"Don't be nervous," I said, looking at her.

She grinned, her fangs glinting. Seeing her like this made me happy, especially after seeing the condition she had been in when we had all rescued Ember. She hadn't been sure how long she'd been kept there, but she already seemed like a different person.

"I actually used to work in the office," she said. "I did a lot of the hiring and stuff. So hopefully, that will work to my advantage."

"I'm surprised you want anything to do with our office," I said.

Sylvia shrugged. "I like Ember and everyone else I've met. It would be nice to work somewhere that I can enjoy."

It *would* be nice.

Not that I didn't enjoy my job, but I wasn't the one getting laid on the clock. I wasn't an idiot. I knew what happened behind some of the closed doors here. I had managed to get the office background music turned up just enough to help muffle the occasional moan— because that was the type of secretary I was. A damn good one.

Instead of getting fucked, I'd been keeping Alex from falling apart, including taking phone calls from executives way above my pay grade.

Then there were all of the rescues we'd done.

I could add rescuing people to my resume at this point.

The elevator chimed, and the door slid open. The two of us stepped out into the hall, and I led Sylvia through the office space and then to Alex's office.

I knocked on the door frame, peeking around the corner. Alex lifted his head, his lightning-blue eyes meeting mine. A shock wave worked through me, and it took every ounce of control to fight back the possessive growl that I wanted to make.

"Hey, Alex," I said, swallowing hard. "I have Sylvia with me."

"Come in," Alex said.

I nodded and went in, followed by Sylvia.

The moment she stepped into the room, I felt the energy immediately change.

Alex froze, his eyes falling on her. He stared at her for a moment as if he saw a ghost, as if she were a monster coming back from his past. His eyes then moved to me, taking me in.

Looking at me the way I wanted him to look at me. Like he was hungry. Like he needed only one thing to live, and I was it.

I sucked in a breath as I caught the scent of his heat. I had been working at this office for months now and had smelled many omega scents. Over and over, and none of them had ever affected me like this.

But *his*? His was different.

This was Alex, and I *wanted* him.

It was addicting. It was a scent I could breathe forever, wanted to breathe forever. I wanted to devour him while giving in to whatever he wanted.

Sylvia gaped, taking a step back. Her six eyes widened, looking from him to me. "No," she said.

"Get out," Alex said, his voice barely above a whisper.

"Alex—"

"Get the fuck out of my office," he snarled, slamming his hand down on the desk.

Sylvia immediately fled, not even giving him a second glance. I could feel her terror, could hear her heart pounding. I could hear his too.

His skin started to flush, but was it his temper or his heat?

The air crackled with electricity, a light blue aura emerging around him like a cerulean halo.

I growled, torn between staying to yell at him or going after Sylvia.

"Leave, Anne," he said, his eyes now glued on his desk. "Please. This is dangerous."

His chest was heaving now, sweat beading on his forehead.

"Go home," I whispered, glaring at him. "Get the fuck out of the office and go home before others catch your scent. Portal out of here, and don't come back until you've taken care of yourself."

"It doesn't work that way," he said, looking up at me.

Fuck. If looks could kill, I would be dead and horny.

"Leave me before I lock you in with me and fuck you until your voice is so hoarse from screaming you have to call in tomorrow," he growled.

"Fuck you," I whispered, turning and leaving.

This was a fucking disaster. An absolute nightmare.

Did this mean...

I paused, looking back at the doorway as a blue light flashed from within his office.

He had left, taking his omega scent with him.

Mate.

My heart started to thrash in my chest, and my breath left me.

It rang through my mind, crystal clear.

He was mine.

She was mine.

Fuck.

The three of us were mates.

CHAPTER THREE

parking garage secrets

SYLVIA

I RODE THE ELEVATOR ALL THE WAY DOWN TO THE parking garage, cursing to myself. I was thankful I was alone and able to let it out.

This had been a fucking nightmare. Alex, the boss who I had been literally thinking about trying to impress for over a week now, had gone into heat right in front of me.

I wanted *nothing* to do with omegas. Nothing. I had already been through enough, and while it wasn't the omegas' fault for all of the things that had happened with Alfred, I still didn't want anything to do with them like that.

I didn't want mates either, and that...that had meant only one thing.

Anne, the sexy secretary, and Alex, the Warts & Claws Inc. boss, were my mates.

The revelation wasn't welcome, but then there was a small part of me that wanted it. There was a little voice inside my head telling me they were the ones for me and that I could finally be loved.

I could finally love.

I wasn't an ancient monster. I hadn't been around for a few hundred years. I was only twenty-six and I was still figuring out my place in the world. Plus, all of the terrible things that had happened recently certainly hadn't helped much.

Still, there was that voice... that thought.

I wanted them both. I wanted Alex. I wanted Anne. I wanted to find out what it would be like to be with the two of them together, to be with them alone.

The doors slid open, and I stepped out into the garage, only to damn near run straight into the devil himself.

"Fuck," we both said, immediately taking a step back from each other.

Alex covered his mouth, his lightning-blue eyes burning. His dark hair was now disheveled, and gone was the glamour of a man in control.

He looked terrified of me, which wasn't comforting. I wanted him to look at me like I was his.

I want him. He's mine.

If I could have slapped myself for thinking that, I would have.

"Sorry," he whispered, taking a step back. "I'm just going to my car to leave. I'm sorry, Sylvia. I was an asshole. I can't control this."

"Just stay away," I said, stepping back from him.

I didn't want him to stay away. In fact, I wanted to pull him close. I wanted to trap him in a web and find out what an omega in heat meant, but that was insane.

What would happen if I shoved him against a car and

went to my knees? What would happen if the two of us ran away together?

Now I was getting ridiculous.

Alex lingered for a moment, sliding his hands into his pockets. "I'm sorry," he said again, taking a breath.

"I have already been through enough," I said, feeling a need to explain myself. Why? I didn't owe him anything. "And witches make me nervous."

He let out a dry laugh. A bitter one. "Witches make me nervous, and I am one. No, you don't deserve to go through anything else. And while I can't control this...reaction... I'll go home and try to figure it out."

"Can you?" I asked.

I shouldn't ask that. Now, the two of us were standing in the parking garage, talking like two awkward younglings. Still, I couldn't resist.

I wanted to know.

"Can I *what?*" he asked, his gaze meeting mine.

"Can you figure this out alone?" I asked.

His lips parted, his brows drawing together. "I don't know," he answered honestly. "I've never gone into heat like this. I'm..." His words trailed off, and I could practically see the wave of need that rushed over him. His cheeks reddened, a pant leaving him.

"Fuck," he whispered.

He looked like he was in pain. *Suffering.*

He waved his hand and then turned around in the middle of our conversation and walked away. His steps were hurried, and I watched as he walked across the parking garage to his car, got in and slammed the door, and then peeled away.

I didn't want him to go. I wanted him to stay. Fuck.

I did not come in this morning thinking this would be

how my day would go. I had hoped I would walk into this office and land a nice interview, and be able to go back to having a normal life. A life that involved monsters and witches, but in a way that was good.

This has been a disaster.

Still, I felt an ache in my chest. Watching him go had made me only want him more.

The elevator doors slid open again, and out came Anne. I looked up at her, and she looked at me.

"He just left," I whispered.

Anne looked angry. Her eyes were golden with diamond-shaped pupils, and they burned like hellfire.

The snakes that surrounded her head had unraveled, making her appear like she had long luscious locks, except they ended in snakeheads. She was disheveled, her muscles tense.

She came to me and, to my surprise, pushed me against the parking garage wall with a hiss.

"Anne," I gasped, but I didn't stop her.

I'd had a crush on her since I met her. She was the one who had been there for me when I'd been rescued from the office. She had dressed my wounds and made the calls to people who could help. Between her and Ember, they had helped me get back on my legs.

I drew in a shaky breath, taking in her scent.

"Tell me no," Anne whispered.

"I won't tell you no," I said.

Anne sighed and then leaned forward, her lips meeting mine. I groaned, immediately melting against her. My second set of hands settled on her hips, my spider legs wrapping around her body to draw her closer.

She groaned, her tongue meeting mine. She pushed me up against the wall a little bit harder, her hands gliding down my hips. The taste of her was refreshing, but I wanted more. I wanted to do a lot more that wasn't acceptable to happen in a parking garage at work.

I let out a growl and then drew back. "Fuck. We're fucked."

"We are," she rasped, kissing me again.

Her tongue met mine again, and I groaned, feeling my pussy pulse. The scent of Alex's heat still lingered, driving me crazy.

All I could think about was what it would be like to be with both of them at the same time. Alex's heat would drive us crazy, and I wanted to feel that. I wanted to submit to both of them, to give in to whatever they wanted. It had been so long since I'd been with someone, and there was an ache inside my chest that went away when she touched me.

Anne's hands hiked up my dress, her fingers dipping lower. I groaned, breaking our kiss to let my head fall back.

"We'll get caught," I gasped.

"I don't care," she said, her lips trailing down my neck. "I've wanted to taste you since we met and fuck it. I want my own happy ending in this fucking office."

I wasn't sure what she meant exactly, but my thoughts flew out of my head as her fingers found my clit through my underwear. I cried out, my hips bucking as she began to rub me through the fabric.

"That's a good girl," Anne whispered in my ear.

Oh fuck. Fuck, I was a goner.

All concerns about breaking protocol, all reservations about not giving in to what I wanted with her— all of it disintegrated at her words.

She sucked on the curve of my neck, her fingers driving me wild. I let out another cry as a flash of pleasure worked through me.

"Cum," she whispered. "Cum for me, Sylvia, and then we're going to go finish the new hire paperwork."

Her fingers moved faster, driving me closer and closer to the edge. I had no control and couldn't stop her from making me cum. There was nothing I could do. I was hers.

The tips of her fangs teased my skin, and the threat of being bitten was enough to make me crumble.

"Please," I gasped.

"Louder," she growled.

"Please!" I cried, my voice echoing through the garage.

She yanked the shoulder of my dress down, kissing down my chest. Her tongue traced over my markings, all the way down to my exposed breasts.

With a possessive growl, her fangs lengthened, and she sank them into my nipple, sucking hard.

I screamed, forgetting where we were. Forgetting that anyone could walk up on us.

I came hard, my orgasm burning through me. I gasped as my hips jerked, my muscles tensing at the climax, only relaxing as I started to come down.

I collapsed against the wall, panting as Anne pulled her hands away from my pussy, fixed my dress, and then pulled her fangs free of my breast. She swiped her tongue over the marks, but they were already healing.

"Anne," I whispered raggedly.

She looked up at me, licking her lips.

"Can we do that again after work?"

She laughed, fixing the rest of my dress before leaning up to kiss my cheek. "Yes," she said. "Fuck. I really just did that."

"You did," I said, swallowing hard.

"Paperwork and surviving today. We'll figure out Alex tomorrow."

I took a deep breath and let it out. "I didn't want anything to do with witches."

Anne raised a brow. "Do you still want that?"

"No," I admitted.

She smirked. "Right. Well, let's go sign some papers."

CHAPTER FOUR
talk dirty to me

ALEX

I stroked my cock harder, letting out a pained grunt. My body felt like it was on fire, and none of the potions or spells I'd tried had worked. Nothing was working.

I was fucking dying.

I had barely made it home. In fact, by the time I had gotten home, my cock had been hard, and I'd had precum staining my pants.

I gripped the blankets beneath me, thrusting my hips up helplessly. My hand wouldn't do it. None of the toys would either.

Nothing was helping.

I could cum, but it wasn't satisfying.

I could orgasm, but it only left me more needy. More hungry.

"Fuck," I cried.

Sweat covered my body, my muscles tensed.

This was a nightmare. My attraction to Anne had gone from something I could barely suppress to a full on obsession. And then there was Sylvia.

I had seen her before. I had met her before. So why now? Why was I going into heat now?

It was them together.

I thrust into my hand harder at the thought, letting out a heated groan. I was a mess, and this was inappropriate.

I'd let other romances happen in the office without any issues, but I couldn't pursue one. I was the boss, and even if my secretary made me want to...

My breaths became harsher, my hips jerking faster.

"Fuck," I whimpered.

Just the thought of her. It was enough to have me whimpering like this was my first time in heat.

My thoughts roamed to Sylvia.

Fucking hell, maybe I had a thing for monster women.

My breaths came faster, but it still wasn't enough.

Nothing was enough.

I needed to hear her voice.

My eyes opened, and I sat up, reaching for my phone. The hours had flown by, and it was already 4 p.m.

Which meant Anne would be at her desk.

Which meant I could hear her voice.

Fuck it. I had already been masturbating for almost six hours.

I opened up my contact list and hit Warts & Claws Inc. The dial tone made me moan.

I was only moments from hearing her voice.

"Thank you for calling Warts and Claws Inc., this is Anne. How may I help you?"

I was silent for a moment. I was such a pervert doing this to her, but I couldn't help it.

The sound of her voice was heaven.

"Hello? This is Anne. How can I help you?"

"Anne," I whispered.

I could hear her hiss. "*Alex?*"

"I had to hear you," I gasped. "I'm sorry."

I was already stroking my cock again. I knew she was mad at me. She had every right to be.

"Alex," Anne hissed, her voice dropping. "Alex, what the fuck?"

"I had to," I groaned.

"For fuck's sake. Are you touching yourself right now?"

"Yes," I moaned. "Anne, I need you. I've wanted you for so fucking long, and then this morning..."

"Was a disaster," Anne snapped. "An absolute disaster."

"I'm sorry," I whimpered. "I couldn't control myself. I wanted both of you. The moment you both came into the office, I immediately went into heat. It *hurts*."

Anne was quiet for a moment. "You're in pain?"

"Yes, I'm in pain," I said. "I've been touching myself for six hours, and it doesn't matter how many times I cum. I ache to be buried inside of you, to fucking taste you. My entire body hurts because I'm not with you."

Anne sucked in a breath. "So you called me? At work?"

"Who's going to fire you?" I asked.

She let out a chuckle. "Okay. Is this a command from you, Boss?"

"Yes," I said. "Please, Anne. Talk dirty to me."

"You're so desperate," she whispered. "Desperate to hear me."

"I am," I groaned. "You have no idea, Anne."

"Mm. Do you want to hear about what I did to Sylvia earlier?"

"Yes," I gasped.

"Spit on your cock first," Anne whispered.

I grunted and sat up slightly, spitting onto the tip of my cock. It slid down the head, and I gasped as I rubbed it all over my shaft.

"Good," Anne said. "After you left, I pinned Sylvia against the wall in the parking garage. She was so wet. Needy."

I groaned, stroking my cock again. My entire body was burning with lust, my skin emitting a soft blue glow. My room was dark and quiet. The only sound was my cock being stroked.

"Please," I rasped. "Tell me more."

"We kissed, and she tasted so good. Sweet. Her body was soft, and I hiked up her dress. You'd like to do that too, wouldn't you?"

"Fuck," I gasped, shivering. The idea of bending them both over my desk… "Yes. I want to do that so badly."

"You're such a perv," she teased. "Such a bad boss, too. But I hiked her dress up and began to rub her clit while we kissed. She was practically dripping for me. She was wearing black lace panties too. Maybe I should steal them from her and drop them off on your doorstep after work."

"Anne," I breathed. "This is torture."

She giggled again, dropping her voice lower. "She came so well for me, Alex. Especially when I sank my fangs into her soft breast. I tasted her sweet blood, all while making her scream. And then, I hired her."

"Fuck," I gasped. I was shocked. Anne was a sweetheart, and yet she was naughty. "You're so…"

"Bad?" she teased.

"Good," I grunted.

"I'm glad you think so. Hmm. I'll drop the underwear off tonight, and you can fuck your cock with it."

"Anne," I groaned. "You're going to drive me insane."

"Good. I think it'll be good for you. Now, cum for me so I can get back to work."

She was so demanding, but I was putty in her hands. I was so used to being the boss, to being in control and making all the decisions.

To have her tell me what to do was irresistible.

"Cum, Alex. You fucking omega slut."

I grunted and pumped my cock harder, gasping as I did what she asked. Her growl was what sent me over the edge, and I cried out, hot cum shooting from my cock.

It filled my hand, dripping down my shaft. I felt a rush of relief, letting out a breath.

"Did that help your pain?"

"Yes," I whispered, my mind spinning. "Come over tonight."

"I would, but I have a date with the new hire," she said.

"Then both of you come over," I rasped.

"No. I'd like to spend some time getting to know her."

"Anne," I whined. "Please."

"You're cute when you're desperate. I will let you know. We'll put a pin in it for now."

"Fuck," I sighed.

"I'll talk to you later. Get some sleep."

"Thank you," I whispered.

The line clicked, ending the call.

My chest rose and fell, my body buzzing from cumming so hard.

I hadn't expected her to be so...

Dominant.

But I liked it.

I hoped that she dropped Sylvia's panties off tonight. The things I would do... Fuck.

I had a thing for lingerie. Pantyhose. Everything and anything like that.

I closed my eyes with a sigh. My body still felt like it was on fire, but it was a little better than it had been.

I hoped that both of them came over tonight.

If not, I would go to the office in the morning.

I had to see them again.

CHAPTER FIVE
tuesday orientation

ANNE

I'd left Alex hanging last night and the guilt was eating me alive.

In my defense, Sylvia and I hadn't been able to see each other anyway. The last hour at the office yesterday had turned into an entire series of unfortunate events. Art had been fucking helpless without Inferna and Alex around, and we'd ended up having to work overtime in order to finish up some of the problems that had happened throughout the day.

One of them being, we had a project due this week and we were only halfway finished with it.

Another one being that Alex's meeting with the other company had been done by Art and me, and while we had survived it, Inferna or Alex were needed.

At least Inferna would be back today. I hoped she had a good three day weekend, but this office was falling apart, and it was above my pay grade to glue it back together.

I set my bag down on my desk, glancing at the clock next to my stack of papers. It was 7:30 a.m. and come hell or high water, I would be out of this place early tonight.

Still...

I grabbed my phone, checking my messages. I had texted Sylvia last night and she had been understanding about me working late, but I still felt bad. Not to mention, Alex was in heat.

Was he okay? Should I have called him?

I swallowed hard, thinking about my phone call with him yesterday.

Last night had been hell for that reason too. While I had been working to solve problems that weren't even mine, I'd been trying not to think about his helpless moans or the way he had cum for me. I had been trying not to think about the way Sylvia had cum on my fingers, and how good she fucking tasted.

I had been trying not to think about any of those things, and had failed, which meant yesterday had been torture for me too. All of the taunting during our phone call, and I'd ended up being the one with blue balls. Then, to make things worse, I'd gotten home ready to use all my toys and had instead passed out on the couch.

At least I would see Sylvia again today. I had her coming in for orientation, and would be able to spend more time with her. Maybe tonight, we could go see Alex after work and make sure he was alive.

I let out a little huff, seeing that I had no more text messages. I set my phone down, and then turned, heading for the elevators. I hit the button for the next floor, needing to grab files from Alex's desk. I waited for the doors to slide open before stepping inside, riding up to the next floor in peace.

The moment the doors slid open, the scent of my boss hit me. I let out a helpless groan, immediately moving out into the hallway.

Fuck. Surely he had not been dumb enough to come to work.

I hissed as I marched straight to his office, ready to fight. Ready to send him home. I rounded the corner into his office, only to be shoved against the wall by him.

"Alex," I growled.

I'd forgotten how tall he was until now. I looked up at him, feeling a shiver work up my spine. He was wearing a button-down, but his tie was missing and his shirt wasn't pressed like normal. His dark hair was unkempt, his skin burning with heat.

The scent of him hit me again and I breathed him in, letting out a breath.

His eyes burned, his arm pressing against the wall above me. His cock was hard in his pants against me, his chest rising with rapid breaths like he'd just run a race.

"Good morning," he whispered, his voice hoarse. Broken.

He was desperate. Desperate for my touch, to hear me, to see me.

Knowing that made me feel weak.

"I meant to check on you last night," I whispered, swallowing hard. "I'm sorry I teased you and never checked in, that was rude."

"Don't be sorry for that," he said. "I'm here now. I had to see you, Anne."

"We're at work," I hissed.

"Anne," he growled. "I don't care *where* we are. I don't care who sees us. No one is going to fire me, no matter what I do. I could bend you over my desk and take you, let the whole office hear you scream... and the only one who might get mad at me is Inferna."

"She would," I whispered. "She'd tell you to go home."

"I think she'd tell you to go with me..." His words trailed off, his gaze searching mine.

He lifted his hand, brushing my cheek with the back of his finger.

"Tell me no," he murmured.

"No," I said, "I won't tell you that."

"Then tell me yes."

"Yes," I breathed. "Touch me, Alex."

Yes was the only word he needed. He leaned down, crushing his lips against mine. I felt an electric shock move through me, my arms immediately wrapping around his neck.

I groaned, sliding my hand down to his pants. With the flick of one motion, I undid the button and moved my hand against his cock. He groaned, breaking our kiss for a moment to gasp before capturing my mouth again.

Desire moved through me, a magnetic force I could not resist. After yesterday's phone call, I had been convinced I would be the one to take control, but now...

Alex grunted as he hiked my skirt up, his fingertips sending electric shocks across my skin and scales. I gasped as he went to his knees in front of me.

With the way my anatomy worked, I didn't have a need for underwear, and I was surprised that he found my slit so quickly.

"Have you been with a gorgon before?" I asked, gasping as he ran his fingers over my entrance. I shivered in pleasure, my nipples hardening against my bra.

Alex looked up at me, raising a dark brow. "I like monsters, little viper."

Fuck. No one had ever used a pet name on me before, and I liked it a lot more than I thought I would.

The corner of his mouth tugged into a smile before his tongue dipped inside of me, the tip pushing through my folds.

I covered my mouth just as I cried out, my head falling back. My tail moved, wrapping around the two of us as he began to thrust his tongue in and out.

He drew back for a moment, licking his lips. "Let them down. I know you won't turn me to stone."

"They might bite you," I whispered.

"I don't care," he said. "I want all of you, Anne. Every single part of you. I'm desperate."

I reached up, yanking on the tie that kept the serpents around my head bound together and out of the way. He reached up as they fell down to my shoulders, tugging on my blouse.

"Off with this," he said. "Please."

I nodded, already lifting the hem. The serpents around me hissed, all of them moving as I threw my blouse to the ground. I unhooked my bra too, now fully naked aside from my hiked up skirt in my boss's office.

"Beautiful," he mouthed, his throat bobbing as he swallowed hard.

The way he looked at me— it was as if I were a goddess. Everything about me that had frightened lovers away in the past were the things he cherished.

His palms were smooth as he ran them up my stomach, cupping my breasts. One of the serpents around my head struck at him, leaving a harmless but painful bite on his hand.

He only chuckled, rubbing the pad of his thumb over my nipples.

Fuck. I groaned, my head falling back again. I felt the heat of his breath against my other breast, his tongue flicking out and teasing me.

I was going to cum just from him playing with me. For someone so desperate, he was certainly patient enough.

"Alex," I rasped. "Alex, I want you inside of me."

"Not yet," he said, sucking on my nipple.

I moaned again, my eyes fluttering. He gave me a little bite, drawing a gasp of surprise from me before lowering himself again.

This time he gripped my hips, his fingertips digging into me as he pressed his mouth against my slit. I slid my fingers into his hair as he began to eat me out, feeling a zap on his tongue. His magic was electric, his touch sending shocks through me.

He pulled more cries and pants from me. Everything about his touch turned me on, every little lick and thrust of his tongue sending me closer and closer to the edge.

"Alex," I gasped. "Please."

He pulled back and kissed up my stomach, rising up. He cupped my face, bringing me into another kiss.

I melted even more, tasting him. Drinking in his lust, letting it drive us both crazier.

His hand slid back down my body, two of his fingers slowly pressing inside of me.

I arched against him with a whimper.

"Tell me if that feels good," he said, his voice husky. "I want to know what feels good."

"Aren't you the one in heat?"

He chuckled, moving his fingers gently. He was teasing me, the feeling of them inside me warming me up for something bigger. I gasped as he added his thumb over my clit, rubbing it in small lazy circles.

"I came five times this morning just thinking about you," he said. "Thinking about what you would taste like. What you would feel and look like. And even though I want to fill you up over and over right now, I still want to savor being with you. Your pleasure comes first, little viper."

My breath hitched as his fingers continued to work their magic, my muscles giving small spasms as the pleasure began to build. It was going from small intense stabs to a roaring wave, one that was going to take me down with it.

"I want you to cum before I do, because I want the taste of you on my lips as I fill you with my cock," he breathed.

I couldn't even speak now. The tone of his voice was almost hypnotic, his fingers moving faster. I groaned, gripping his shirt as he continued pushing me.

"Use your words, sweetheart. Does this feel good? Or should I stop?"

He stopped for a moment and my eyes flew open, a growl leaving me. "Bastard."

He smirked and then began to thrust his fingers in and out faster, his thumb moving over my clit. The pleasure came slamming back and I cried out.

"Good," he whispered. "Cum for me. It's all I want right now."

He kept going until my voice echoed through his office, my climax finally crashing into me. I came hard, my entire body tensing as I screamed.

I leaned into the wall with a groan, my blood rushing in my ears as I relaxed. He pulled his fingers free, licking them clean as my chest heaved.

"Fuck," I rasped. "That was intense."

"Good," he said.

I looked down at the bulge in his pants, raising a brow.

"Want some help with that?"

He was about to respond when the sound of the elevator chiming echoed down the hall.

"*Alex*," I said, my eyes widening.

Fuck, we could not be found like this.

"Get dressed," he hissed. "I'll go intercept."

"You can't!" I snapped. "Your cock is hard and you look like you have the fucking flu. Hand me my bra and shirt!"

Alex grabbed them and threw them at me as the sound of footsteps echoed down the hall.

"Fuck," he mumbled. "It's too late. Come here."

He grabbed me, pulling me across the room to a closet door. The two of us tumbled inside, shutting it just as the office door creaked open.

Both of us held our breath, listening.

Whomever it was, I hoped they turned around and left.

CHAPTER SIX
boss's desk

SYLVIA

I stood in my boss's office, the scent of sex lingering. It was like a drug, making my head spin as I took in a deep breath.

My heart was beating loudly, my nerves working through me. I shouldn't have been up here, but I had taken the elevator up anyway.

I hadn't slept last night. I had almost skipped breakfast this morning. I was losing my mind and it was all because of a witch and a gorgon.

I looked around the office, breathing in their scent again. Where in the hell had they gone?

I wanted to see Alex again, even though everything in my right mind told me not to. He was a witch, he had been involved with the people who had captured me, he was someone I couldn't trust. But, I couldn't get him out of my mind.

Then there was Anne. She was unforgettable, even

when she wasn't shoving me against a parking garage wall and making me cum.

I could hear hearts beating.

My ears strained as I listened, focusing on everything around me. I could hear the AC, could hear the vents throughout the building. I could hear the traffic outside too. But above all of that, I could hear the sound of two heartbeats.

"It's just me," I whispered.

I waited, my eyes falling on the door to the closet. I raised a brow, crossing my arms. I could see the edge of a bra strap sticking out from underneath the door.

Under almost any other circumstance it would've been hilarious, but the fact of the matter was, I wanted to be in that closet with them.

The door creaked open, and Anne poked her head around.

"You scared the hell out of us," she hissed. "I thought you were going to be Inferna, or someone else."

I let out a little giggle, leaning against the desk behind me. I gave a shrug as she moved out into the room, Alex tumbling out behind her. Both of them were half dressed, their chests heaving as if they had just run a marathon. They both smelled like sex and arousal.

Alex looked up at me, his cheeks turning bright pink. For a witch who was much older than me, and for someone who was also my boss, he was very cute. Almost painfully so.

His embarrassment made me want to wrap him up in a web and make him cum.

"We meet again," Alex said.

My eyes roamed over his body, falling down to his hard

cock. I could see the outline in his pants, straining against the zipper.

"Indeed," I said. "I... I would be a liar if I said I didn't come up here so that I could see if the two of you were doing exactly this."

Anne snorted as she hooked on her bra, pulling her blouse over her body. She then moved over toward me quickly, pinning me against the desk in one swift motion. I gasped, surprised by her movements.

"So you wanted us to fuck you too?" she asked. "Was cumming yesterday not enough for you?"

I sucked in a breath, not hearing anything now except my own heart. It was beating fast, my pussy already pulsing in the same rhythm.

Alex let out a curse, drawing both of our attention back to him. He looked like he had a fever, his face flushing as he watched the two of us. He covered his mouth, turning away.

"Are you embarrassed?" I snapped.

"No," Anne giggled. "He's turned on. I bet this is a dream come true for him, two monster girls getting frisky on his desk."

"Fuck off," he scoffed, but his threat had no depth to it. He turned to look at us, his eyes darkening. "I'm not going to stop you if you want to do more. But I also need to cum. So if you decide to continue, I will need to take care of myself...."

"Cum while you watch then," Anne said, giving him a devious smile. She looked down at me, raising a brow. "What do you say?"

"Yes," I whispered.

She pushed me back onto the desk, some of the pens and supplies crashing to the floor. I grunted as she gripped my thighs, already parting my legs.

"Go sit in the chair, boss," Anne said, giving his office chair a subtle nod.

Alex let out a little huff, and then crossed the room to his chair. He took a seat right as Anne yanked down my skirt, letting it fall to the floor.

I sucked in a breath as the cool air brushed over my skin, the January chill chasing us inside here. I knew it wouldn't last for long though, her tongue already doing dangerous patterns on the inside of my thigh.

The snakes danced around her head, her eyes locking with mine. My pussy pulsed with need, the scent of the two of them making me feel high. I groaned, leaning my head back with a small gasp.

Alex was right there, already pulling out his cock. His eyes reminded me of lightning, his square jaw clenched as he spat, starting to stroke himself.

"Kiss me," I whispered.

He looked up, his dark brows lifting with surprise.

"Are you sure?" he whispered.

"Yes," I said, eager to taste him. "Unless you don't want me."

He shook his head, his eyes darkening even more. "You have no idea how much I want you, Sylvia."

Just hearing him say my name was enough to make me groan. He leaned down, his lips meeting mine.

It was an interesting angle, considering that I was upside down on his desk. But it proved to be a fun one, our tongues meeting. The taste of him was perfect, and I could even taste... I could taste Anne's cum.

I gasped as he bit my bottom lip right at the same moment Anne brushed her tongue over my clit through my panties.

Anne pulled them down, a crimson lace pair I had worn

because I'd hoped for this to happen. I gasped as her fangs scraped over my skin, sending a thrill through my entire body.

Alex chuckled against me, cupping my face. His touch was sweet, but also edged with a darkness I craved.

He drew back, his breath mingling with mine. "Fuck, you taste good, sweetheart."

"So do you," I moaned.

"Here," Anne said.

I looked up right as she tossed him my panties. Alex caught them, his eyes lighting up.

"Fuck," he growled.

He had an almost guilty look for a moment, but then he held them up to his face, breathing in the scent. Watching him do that turned me on more than I thought possible.

I gasped as Anne buried her face between my legs. The snakes moved around, curling around my thighs. The spider legs that surrounded me moved, three of them reaching for Anne, the other three for Alex.

I let my head fall back, looking up at him again. "Use my mouth," I moaned. "I want to taste your cock."

Alex curled his fingers in my hair, gripping for a moment. He leaned down, his lips brushing over mine again before he moved back.

"Are you sure?"

"I want to. Please," I rasped. "Use my throat while you breathe in the scent of my pussy."

He growled, his eyes burning brighter.

I cried out as Anne buried her tongue inside of me, pleasure racking me. Alex stroked his thumb over my face, parting my lips with it.

I gave his finger a soft bite, enjoying the way he stuttered. He held my panties to his face again, breathing in deep.

I was getting fucked on my boss's desk by his secretary. Fuck.

Anne moved her hand over my pussy, her finger stroking my clit. She drove her tongue deeper, the length of it going further inside of me.

I gasped, only to see Alex stand up tall. He let his pants fall to the floor, his cock springing free. He held the head of it to my lips, pre-cum dripping from the tip. I lapped it up, the taste of him bursting on my tongue.

Fuck. He tasted amazing. I opened my mouth wider, wanting him to fill me completely. He held back for a moment and groaned.

"Are you sure, Sylvia?"

"*Fuck* me," I growled. "Please. Your cum tastes amazing, and I've been thinking about the two of you non-stop since yesterday morning."

Finally, he caved.

He leaned forward, planting his hands on the desktop. More paper scattered as he moved them out of the way. He grunted, the head of his cock pressing against my mouth.

I took him inside, immediately sucking. I wanted him to bury it deep inside my throat. I wanted to take every single inch.

I wanted to taste him, to make him cum.

There were so many things I wanted to do with the two of them that it made my head spin.

I groaned as he began to push more inside of me, giving me a couple more inches. His hips dragged back before he thrust forward again filling me with more of his cock.

Anne's tongue was working magic on me, sending tremors through my body.

Alex gasped as he thrust harder, filling my throat completely. I moaned around him, my eyes rolling back as he began to use me.

The two of them were driving me crazy, driving me closer and closer to the edge. Pleasure worked through my entire body, my muscles tensing.

I loved the feeling of taking them both at the same time, her tongue driving me wild while he fed me his cock.

"You feel so fucking good," Alex grunted. "Fuck, you take my cock so well."

Anne leaned back, pulling her tongue free. She replaced it with two of her fingers, moving them in a motion that hit a spot inside my body that drove me even more wild.

She kept moving them, but I heard her lean up. I felt something move on the desk and squealed around Alex's thrusting cock as I felt my shirt be ripped open.

Alex pulled his cock free for a moment, allowing me to breathe. I grunted as he cradled my head, helping me sit up slightly so I could watch as Anne lifted two binder clips.

She had a wicked look in her eyes, her tongue flicking out to lick her lips.

"How do you feel about pain?" she asked.

The pleasure of pain was a real thing, and it was something I craved more often than not. It had been too long since I had a partner who had been interested in such things too, and it excited me to know she was wanting to do something.

"I love it," I said, biting my lower lip.

My throat ached from taking his cock, and the feeling made me smile.

"I like doing things," I said. "I like doing things that hurt. I like being bound, and I like using my webs on people too. There are times when I like to have things done to me, and as long as I know what my partner likes it's fun to explore together."

"And you?" she asked, looking up at Alex.

He raised a brow, his lips tugging into a dry smile.

"I like giving more than receiving. Which means that I enjoy giving pleasure and also giving pain."

"Well, if you're as good at giving the second as you are at the first, then I think both Sylvia and I will be happy."

"I will do my best," Alex promised. "And maybe I can convince you both to actually come over tonight."

"Yes," I said. "Please. I want to do more."

Both of them nodded, exchanging a knowing look together. Anne then looked down at me, leaning over my body.

Hers was warm against mine, my legs wrapping around her hips. She yanked open my bra, freeing both of my breasts. I gasped as Alex leaned down, dragging his tongue down the marking that decorated my chest and torso. I groaned, the feeling turning me on all over again.

She made me cry out as she thrust her fingers back inside of me. My entire body arched, my pussy pulsing as she used her freehand to clamp one of my nipples with one of the clips.

It felt like one of them was pinching me, and it made me gasp. Alex chuckled against me, and then rose back up, slapping my cheek with his cock.

"I can't wait to feel you," he whispered. "I can't wait to fill you up with my cock, and thrust into your pussy over and over again. And I'm going to do that tonight when we get home."

"Please," I gasped.

"But for now, I want my secretary to make you cum."

She let out a hiss, grinning as she lowered herself back between my legs. The moment the tip of her tongue touched my clit, it was as if I'd been electrocuted.

I cried out, pleasure flashing through me like a heat wave. Alex leaned over me, his fingers running over my breasts. He gave the clip on one of my nipples a tug, causing me to squeal.

"Oh, I like that noise," he growled. "I like hearing you squeal."

She began to suck on my clit, and I cried out. I was so close to the edge.

"I'm so close," I gasped. "I'm so close, please don't stop."

It sounded like a beg. My voice echoed through the office, and I wasn't sure how loud I was getting, nor did I care. Everyone could hear us, everyone could know, and I didn't care so long as I could finally cum.

"Please," I moaned. "Fuck. I want you to cum on me," I gasped.

Where had that come from? I'd never wanted something so much, but the idea of him shooting his cum over me was what I wanted more than anything.

Alex groaned, his hand moving down to his cock and stroking it. He stroked faster and faster. My head spun as I listened to him jack himself off, the scent of him filling me with pleasure. Anne's tongue still circled my clit, and I was so fucking close.

Alex leaned down, taking my other nipple between his teeth. He gave it a gentle bite, and that sent a whole new shockwave through me. Anne rubbed my clit faster, and finally I screamed out as my climax crashed into me.

I felt hot cum shoot out onto my breasts and I gasped, shivering from my orgasm as Alex sprayed his cum over me.

Anne immediately kissed her way up my body, her

tongue lapping up his seed. She growled, pausing for a moment.

"Fuck. This shouldn't taste this good."

She licked more of it up until she planted a kiss on my lips, sharing his cum with me. I groaned because she was right, I wanted more.

I was about to say something, when a sharp knock at the door sent a bolt of sheer panic through my soul.

All three of us looked up.

"Alex!" It was Inferna.

"DO NOT COME IN HERE," Alex bellowed. "I AM BUSY."

"Alex, I swear to the fucking gods," Inferna snarled. "Is Anne in there with you?!"

"No!" he shouted.

"Liar," she snickered. "We need to meet when you're able, I have bad news."

CHAPTER SEVEN
back from hell

ALEX

BEADS OF SWEAT ROLLED OVER MY SKIN.

I leaned over the bathroom sink, trying to catch my breath before I went into the meeting. I gripped the sides of it, looking at myself in the mirror.

Yes. I was definitely in heat, there was no fucking denying that.

My dark brows drew together. I wanted to be back in my office with Sylvia and Anne, doing whatever I wanted to them. The taste of both of them was still on my lips, my body yearning for them.

This was the hardest part about being an omega— and now that I had my mates, it was even worse.

Mates.

The thought chilled me to the bone while setting fire to my soul.

I wanted them more than anything else in this world, but I hated myself.

Fuck.

I heard the door open and looked up, surprised to see Calen. He was in his more witchy form, his skin pale green. Over the last couple of months, he'd become a lot more comfortable in his own skin.

He winced at the sight of me.

Fuck, was it that bad?

"Alex, you should go home," he said.

"I know," I said, swallowing hard.

How many times had I been the one to send an omega witch home? Hell, I'd given lectures on reasons why.

"You're not even wearing your gloves today."

It was true. I'd been lucky I'd managed to even wear pants. I'd been lucky to even be able to make it to the office without cumming on them too.

My thoughts started to turn back to everything that had just happened. To everything I had just done with my new employee and secretary. It was supposed to be wrong, but I certainly didn't regret anything.

I wanted more.

I felt that hunger return. The one that used to drive me towards power and greed except now it was focused on lusting after Sylvia and Anne.

"I will be along soon," I said, my voice sharp. "I just need a few more moments to collect myself."

"You do realize that you're in an office full of monsters," Calen said, raising a brow. "And that you have been the one to send several omegas home when the same situation happened to them?"

"Yes," I snapped. "I do realize that. But none of them was the boss of this company."

"Well, that's why you have Inferna."

"Did she send you?"

"No," he chuckled. "I came here to make sure you were okay."

I was silent for a moment, pressing my lips together. He didn't have to check on me.

"Thanks," I mumbled.

I cranked on the faucet, splashing my face with water. I grabbed a paper towel, and dried it off quickly. I would be able to last for another hour or so, but then I would need to go home. Go home or walk around the office with a hard cock, bringing the attention of every monster in the vicinity to me.

"Alright," I said, turning to face him. "Do I at least look presentable?"

"Sure," Calen said, wincing. "Come on."

I fought the urge to sigh and followed him out of the bathroom, going down the hall to Art's office. Inferna and Art were already inside, and their expressions didn't bode well.

Inferna cleared her throat, her dark hair framing her face. Her tail flicked behind her, the heart shaped end waving like a red flag.

That was a sign that she was irritated, which meant this really was bad news.

"What's wrong?" I asked.

Inferna gave me a flat look. "Shut the door."

I waved my hand, using my magic to shut it as I took a seat.

She leaned back in her chair, letting out a sigh. "I have bad news. And it's not something we could control necessarily, but... well, here it is. One of my uncles is Lucifer."

I immediately scowled. I had never run into Lucifer himself, but I had heard plenty of things over the years. I'd also heard that he'd settled down not too far from here and had turned from his evil ways.

"Lucifer is good," Inferna said. "Well, as good as he can be. But he's still mischievous and there are times when he still does things that cause a headache."

I didn't like where this was going.

"I guess about three weeks ago, he got a phone call from hell. I don't even know how that works. But he got a call from Alfred. Apparently uncle Lucy owed him a favor, and repaid it. He sent help and broke him out of hell."

Ice immediately filled my veins, the blood draining from my face. I felt my chest squeeze, panic edging up.

"I'm sorry," Inferna said. "The good news is, uncle Lucy is family so he immediately told us about it. He told the Barista, and the Barista called my dad. And my dad called me. Yesterday, I got the phone call while at home."

"Fuck," I whispered, leaning back in my seat. "Fuck. This is bad."

"It is," she said, grimacing. "If it's any consolation, I think Lucy hasn't been flogged now for a few weeks."

"Isn't that....isn't that a good thing?"

"No," she snickered.

I raised a brow but didn't say anything, still reeling from the news.

I had believed it was over.

I had been living the last few weeks finally free of the monster who had been determined to ruin my life. Who had been determined to hurt so many witches and monsters alike.

My gut twisted as I thought about him coming back.

I was in heat now.

It was only a matter of time. And now that I was in heat because of Anne and Sylvia...

"They're in danger," I whispered.

"Who?" Art asked.

"Anne and Sylvia."

Art and Calen cocked their heads while Inferna only raised a brow.

"Is that who I smelled in your office?"

I waved my hand, refusing to answer that. "I am in heat right now."

"Right," Art said, "Which brings up the next thing. Why are you here at work? You've spent the last few months being so adamant that any omega witch in heat takes time off, but here you are. You're being an idiot."

"Candid," I muttered. "But true. I had to see Anne."

"Ah," Inferna said. "Hmmm.... I like Anne a lot. And Sylvia has been hurt from Alfred too."

"We all have," Calen whispered.

I looked over at him, giving a small nod. "I'm sorry. Most of this is my fault. But, I thought it was over."

"We thought it was too," Inferna said. "It's unfortunate he had a favor to call on."

"It's fortunate that we had a heads up," Art said.

It was. Now, I knew I had to be infinitely more careful. I had to figure out how to protect Anne and Sylvia without completely succumbing to my heat.

Which was damn near impossible.

Even the thought of them right now, even with the terrible news looming over our heads, sent a pang of need through me.

"Go home," Inferna said. "You're a strong witch. Put up spells. I'm sure all of our witches would be willing to reinforce them too. Spend a couple days with Anne and Sylvia, fuck a lot, break your heat, and then we will track down

Alfred. I'm sure he's not far, but I think we still have a little bit of time."

Did we? Did we have any time? How did I know he wasn't already waiting for me?

"Why does he hate you so much?" Inferna asked.

"Because he wanted me," I said, swallowing hard. "And I didn't want him."

Inferna groaned. "For fuck's sake. Someone teach monsters that rejection is okay."

Art and Calen both snorted.

"I will handle it," I said, standing up from my chair.

Inferna stood too, meeting me eye to eye. "Not alone," she said firmly. "Promise me you will do what I just said."

"I'm the—"

"Don't you fucking say it," she said.

I glared at her for a moment, but then I couldn't help but smile. She was a force to be reckoned with and I respected the hell out of her.

"You're very direct sometimes," I said.

"And you're very stupid sometimes. Do not put Anne or Sylvia in jeopardy because you can't listen to directions, Alex. I like them both."

"I like them both too," I said, walking around the chair to the door. I paused, holding the handle. "I'm going home. If you need me, call."

"I will," Inferna said, crossing her arms. "If anything happens, please let us know."

"I will," I promised.

And that was one I would keep.

I was tired of fighting alone. It didn't help anything.

"We've taken him down once," Art said, looking around the room. "We can do it again."

It was true, but now that he had crawled out of hell, he would be ten times harder to deal with.

I nodded and then opened the door, sliding out into the main office. I saw Anne at her desk, Sylvia leaning against it. Both of their heads turned, gazes holding mine.

I went to them, pressing my lips together. "Come home with me," I said. "Please."

They both nodded, and the three of us headed to the elevators.

CHAPTER EIGHT
dinner

ANNE

I ALREADY WANTED MORE. I WAS ALREADY DESPERATE to touch him again, to feel Sylvia writhing beneath me. We made it to Alex's house within a few minutes, and I wasn't surprised that it was so close by.

Alex opened the front door and I groaned as I stepped in, immediately surrounded by the scent of him. Sylvia let out a breath, looking around.

"It's... It's kind of a mess," he muttered, his cheeks turning red.

It was a mess, but mostly because it was obvious he really had been going crazy yesterday. There were blankets on his couch, on the floor, mounds of pillows. There was the tinge of magic in the air, an almost electrical feel to it.

His house was cozier than I had expected, which was a nice surprise.

"You live alone?" I asked.

"Yeah," Alex said, giving me a thoughtful smile. He

hung his jacket on a coat rack next to the doorway, slipping off his shoes.

It was warm in here too. The world outside fell away, all of my worries slowly leaving.

This morning had been crazy. Hell, the last couple of days had been, but...

I wanted this.

I wanted him. I wanted Sylvia. I wanted to explore the passion and desire between the three of us.

Sylvia looked around and then smiled. "I like it. It suits you."

I could see the doorway from here to his office, catching a glimpse of many books, scattered papers, and a desk that looked like it would have belonged to a writer a couple hundred years ago.

Alex let out a soft groan. I looked at him, catching a wave of his scent. He closed his eyes for a moment, very obviously trying to suppress it.

I looked at Sylvia, not surprised to see that she wore a soft expression. Her long black hair went down to her waist, having unraveled after all of our office shenanigans.

"Alex," I whispered. "What do you want right now?"

Alex opened his eyes, giving us a hungry look. "I want both of you."

"You should eat first," Sylvia said. "I can hear your stomach."

Alex looked down, frowning. "I don't think I ate today. Or yesterday, for that matter."

Sylvia and I both hissed, horrified.

"Idiot," I mumbled, already moving to the kitchen. "Do I need to do everything for you outside of work too?"

"No," he said. "Of course not! I can—"

"I'm teasing," I said, going to his fridge.

Alex made a noise. "I haven't had a chance to shop."

I opened his fridge, surveying what he had. There were some items that might make an okay breakfast, but...

"Yeah," I said, shutting the door. "I can see that."

Sylvia laughed now. "We can order in. Also, are you going to tell us what Inferna told you now?"

I turned to look at the two of them. Alex's expression wasn't a good sign. He ran his fingers through his dark hair nervously, wincing.

I held up my hand. "Let's order some food first," I said. "And then we can talk about it over dinner. And then we can finally see just how far we can go now that we don't have to be quiet in the office."

Both of them nodded, and I pulled my phone from my pocket, pulling up an ordering app. Within a few minutes, the three of us managed to order some food, and found ourselves sitting on the couch together.

I had half expected this to be awkward, but it wasn't. It felt right.

Alex was so different outside of the office, and I watched as he completely relaxed between us. He grabbed one of his blankets, pulling it around himself like a little shield

I took a deep breath, his scent comforting me.

It also turned me on.

I knew he had to be hurting at this point, having not come now for at least a couple of hours.

One of Sylvia's spider legs slid over my shoulder, moving around me. I looked over at her, and winked. She was gorgeous, and I wanted to hear her begging to be fucked.

The thought made me swallow hard.

How many scenarios had run through my head since Monday morning? It was countless.

I wanted to see what she looked like more shifted too. I knew she was holding on to the rest of her form, and I wanted to see the more monster side of her.

Alex relaxed, drawing in a soft breath. His cheeks were flushed, his skin giving off a soft glow. I looked over his body, seeing the outline of his cock against the blanket wrapped around him.

He was already hard.

"So needy," I whispered, lifting my hand. "May I?"

Alex nodded, a breath leaving his parted lips.

I slid my hand under the blanket, running my fingertips over his bulge. He immediately gasped, his head falling back against the couch cushion.

His hands curled into fists as his breath hitched.

"Anne," he whispered.

Fuck. My name falling from his lips made my pussy throb.

Sylvia let out a soft feminine chuckle, sliding her hand up his chest and griping his face. He turned, the two of them kissing.

I licked my lips as I watched them for a moment, not ashamed of how much that turned me on to see them together.

I gave his cock a soft squeeze, which immediately caused his hips to buck. I slid down to the floor in front of him, pushing his knees apart and the blanket to the side. Alex groaned as I undid his belt and then button and zipper, reaching in and pulling his cock free.

I pulled his pants all the way down and then leaned forward, taking the head of his cock between my lips. He gasped, his hips thrusting up with a helpless moan.

The taste of him made me moan. I swirled my tongue over the tip, dragging my nails down his thighs.

His hips thrust up again, his cock filling more of my mouth.

I wanted him to use me. To throat fuck me hard enough that tears were steaming down my cheeks.

Sylvia held his head still, their tongues fighting for dominance. I began to suck, gripping the bottom of his shaft. His cock was huge, especially given that he wasn't a monster. It was a little over 9 inches, and the perfect thickness.

I swiped my tongue over the bead of precum, the taste making me groan.

His cum must have been magic too. There was something about it, something about him beyond the fact that he turned me on so much. His scent was like a drug, and his taste was addicting.

I took his cock all the way down my throat and he cried out, his hips thrusting up again. I choked on it, already feeling myself get wet.

"I'm going to cum," he gasped. "I can't stop."

I pulled off for a moment, licking my lips. "Cum, then. Don't stop yourself. I want to taste you, *Boss*."

Sylvia ripped open his shirt, kissing his chest as I took his cock in my mouth again. Alex let out a loud cry, his hips thrusting up again.

I sucked harder, stroking his cock faster. I wanted him to fill my mouth, to taste him.

His hips begin to move up and down, and I raked my nails down his thighs. He gasped, losing himself to us.

Sylvia sucked on one of his nipples, which to my surprise, immediately made him cum.

He grunted, his hot cum shooting down my throat. His hips jerked, his hands gripping the blankets as he filled me.

I swallowed, my head swimming as I leaned back. I licked my lips, my lips buzzing with satisfaction.

"Fuck," he groaned. "Fuck. The two of you will be the death of me."

Sylvia grinned. "Maybe that's what we want."

"Oh yeah?" he asked with a dazed smirk. "To fuck me so much I simply die?"

"Yep," she teased.

He shook his head, but he was smiling.

My phone went off, a notification that our food was here.

I giggled and then rose up, moving for the door. "That should hold you for dinner."

I grabbed our food from the porch and brought it inside.

"We can sit here and eat," Sylvia said. "That way you can stay with your nest."

Alex was quiet for a moment, and then nodded. "Thank you."

I put the food down on the coffee table, pulling everything out. We'd ordered from a restaurant that secretly served monsters, which meant that Sylvia and I had been able to get food we actually liked. I put everything out, the three of us settling around.

Alex wrapped the blanket around himself again, his cheeks still flushed with heat.

I wondered how many times Sylvia and I would need to make him cum before it broke.

"Inferna told me that Alfred got out of hell," Alex sighed. "Someone let him out. Well, someone being Lucifer, who is apparently her uncle."

"Fuck," I said.

Sylvia was silent, the color draining from her face.

Alex looked over at her, his eyes softening. "He won't get you again, love. I promise. Neither one of you will be harmed by him."

I hoped that would be true, although I wasn't worried about myself as much as Alex and Sylvia. So far, I'd managed to stay out of his crossfire.

"Inferna wants me to stay home. And if both of you are willing to, I'd like for you to stay with me. She suggested breaking my heat and then we can all track him down."

"Will he wait that long to do something?" I asked.

"We have no way of knowing," he sighed. "I'm sorry. It's bad news. And I don't want either one of you to feel trapped here."

"If I didn't want to be here right now, I wouldn't be," Sylvia said, her tone surprising me.

Alex looked at her, studying her the same way I did. I still wasn't sure of all the things that she had endured when dealing with Alfred and everything else. She had been trapped there.

Sylvia let out a little growl, standing up. "I need a moment."

"Okay," Alex said. "You can use my office or bedroom. Or even backyard," he said. "It's small but nice."

We watched as she left, going to the sliding glass door and slipping outside.

Alex stopped eating, his eyes darkening some. "I hate how much damage I've caused."

"Have you caused this?" I asked, my tone sharp. "Did you hurt her? Was that your purpose?"

"No," he gasped. "No, of course not."

"You can't control Alfred. He's an evil bastard. Jealous. He likes to hurt others. That's not your fault, Alex."

"I know that his actions aren't my fault, but I feel like I could have stopped him sooner. I should have stopped him sooner. After all these years, he still haunts me. He still causes problems for everyone and all because I simply wouldn't give in to him."

I let out a sigh, taking a bite of my food. "I don't know how to convince you that you're a victim too, but you are. And you can't take responsibility for the things he has chosen to do. But, you can for the things you have done. And you've been trying. I've been working with you for months, and you've finally stopped lying. You've been a huge help to the omegas who have come to the office. You actively give out raises, actively help employees get the help that they need. You're a bit flighty sometimes but you're still a good boss, and Inferna balances you out well."

He was silent for a moment. He then looked up at me, tilting his head to the side. "Have you paid that close attention?"

"More than you know," I mumbled.

He nodded, finally taking another bite of his food.

The glass door slid open and Sylvia came back inside, coming back to sit down at the table.

"I needed to think for a moment," she said. "I thought he was dead and finding out that he isn't is difficult. But Alex, I'm here for you. I'm here with you by my own choice and I don't plan on leaving."

"I am too," I said. "You know I would leave if I didn't want to be here."

"True," Alex said. "I know that. Thanks, you both."

"Plus," Sylvia snickered. "I think we both get to have

some fun from it. Maybe we can do some new things tonight."

"Like what?" I asked, curious.

"We need a safeword," Alex chuckled. "For everything."

"And we should talk about limits," I said. "And then see what's on your mind, little spider."

Sylvia smirked. "Agreed. I think that sounds like a plan."

CHAPTER NINE

mating

SYLVIA

Our safeword was 'red'. By the end of our conversation about what we all liked, the three of us were all ready to go. I was turned on, my body aching to be touched again.

What I wanted was to tie Alex up and for him to allow Anne and me to make him cum however we wanted. He agreed to try that, even though he likes a more dominant position. Anne had brought up a good point though, talking about how even though he would be tied up, his mindset could still be that he was the top. It simply depended on what we wanted.

But, before all of that, we wanted to just fuck. I was so desperate to be filled with his cock. I was so wet and needy, my body burning for them both. I wanted to see him take Anne too, to lick his cum out of her cunt.

Alex pushed me back on the bed, parting my thighs. I gasped as he kissed his way up to my pussy, flicking the tip of his tongue over my clit. I groaned, my body arching up on the mattress. I was surrounded by his scent, his blanket soft and comforting.

Anne leaned down, our lips meeting in a hungry kiss. The sun had set, and the room was dark, allowing me to focus on the sounds the three of us made.

Heat ran through my body, need curling through me. I was desperate for them both, aching to cum already.

Fuck. Alex flicked his tongue over my clit again, the touch making me cry out.

"Does this feel good?" Alex asked.

"Yes," I rasped, my fingers gripping the blanket underneath us.

I breathed in his scent, his heat mixing with the sweetness of Anne.

"Just wait," Anne chuckled, pulling my blouse free. "Just wait until you feel his tongue inside of you."

Her diamond pupils expanded as she freed my breasts, her tongue running over her soft lips.

"Beautiful," she whispered. "Stunning."

I felt myself melt.

I moaned as I felt Alex's breath against my pussy. He pushed my thighs apart farther, and I let out a little gasp as he ran his tongue over my clit again, and then down to my slit.

Oh fuck.

I groaned as his tongue slipped inside of me, tasting me. Teasing me.

"Alex," I breathed.

I felt the monstrous part of me rise up for a moment, the part of me that wanted to shift completely. To let myself truly be a monster.

No.

I had to stay in control.

Anne moved over my chest and I grabbed her hips, bringing her slit to my face. My other set of hands reached up and grabbed her breasts, teasing her nipples.

She gasped as I began to play with her, pushing my tongue inside of her. The taste of her was perfect, and I groaned as I thrust my tongue in and out.

The noises she made— they made me even more wet. Alex licked me, his tongue brushing over my entrance before plunging inside.

I arched up with a groan, an electric shock moving through my body. Everything about this felt right, and I was so fucking desperate for more. Their touch, their moans, the heat we all shared— all of it was perfect.

I slipped my thumb over Anne's clit, rubbing it as I ate her out. She cried out, her voice echoing through the room.

It was getting harder and harder to focus, pleasure building up inside of me. Alex was determined to make me cum, his tongue sending waves through me.

Anne cried out again, so close to cumming. I wanted her to cum, to orgasm on my tongue while I came on Alex's.

I grunted as I continue to eat her out, my body arching against Alex. Anne let out a helpless growl, her hips moving against my face.

"I'm going to cum," she rasped.

I held her tighter, my tongue moving faster. Pleasure burned through me, getting hotter and hotter until finally— the two of us cried out together.

I kept my tongue buried inside of her even as I came, tasting the essence of her orgasm. Alex groaned, his fingers digging into my skin as he lapped up every drop from me.

Anne slowly pulled away, melting onto the bed with a gasp. My head was spinning, my lips wet from her.

My hearts pumped, my blood rushing from the pleasure.

Anne had been right, Alex was damn good.

He kissed up my stomach, his beard scratching my skin. I sucked in a breath as he paused, taking one of my nipples between his teeth.

Anne and I both watched him, enchanted. His cock was throbbing between his legs, his body giving off an electric glow. His eyes burned in the darkness, his energy magnetic.

Anne reached down, her hand cupping his face. "I want to see your real form, witch."

Real form? I was curious. I lifted my head, licking my lips.

Alex sat back for a moment, cocking his head. "Not yet."

"You think you'll frighten us?" Anne giggled.

"You won't," I whispered.

He gave me a soft smile. "Mm. I don't go into that form very often."

"Maybe it will help your heat," Anne said. "But you don't have to."

"Perhaps it would," he chuckled. "At some point, I promise I will. But... I become more of a monster then."

I raised a brow. "Are monsters that bad?"

"Oh yes," he teased, leaning down again. "They're terrible. Especially monster girls."

I gasped as he took my breast into his mouth, giving me a gentle but sharp bite.

"So terrible," he chuckled, kissing back up my chest.

I felt the tip of Anne's tail curl around my ankle, tugging my legs apart. Alex moved between them, his hands gripping my thighs and pushing them back.

Alex leaned down, his lips brushing over my ear. "I'm

going to fuck you first and fill you with my cum. And then I'm going to fill Anne until she stops being so demanding and bossy."

"Bossy?" she sniffed. "Oh, you mean you'll actually tell me what to do?"

I laughed, enjoying their banter. Alex gave her a look, one that had even her swallowing hard.

She stuck her tongue out and then moved off the bed, sitting in a chair that was against the wall. "I want to watch this," she said, running her tongue over her lips. "Let's see how many times Alex can actually cum tonight."

"Anne, I swear," he chuckled. "Maybe I will spank you before I fuck you."

"If you're strong enough to hold me down."

"Maybe I'll help him," I teased.

"Traitor," she said, grinning.

The three of us laughed, which somehow made everything even hotter. I was both relaxed and tense, wanting him to fill me with his cum.

He grabbed my upper set of arms, pushing them back above my head. He pinned my wrists into the pillow, the tip of his cock brushing against me.

I groaned, feeling another wave of heat rush through me.

"Beg me," he whispered, looking down at me.

I let out a breath, staring up at him. He held my gaze, the feeling of his magic brushing over me. There was a power to him that I hadn't expected, one that drew me in like a moth to a flame.

"Please," I whispered.

"Please what?" he asked.

He gazed down at me like I was the center of the

universe. He was patient, waiting for me to beg exactly how he wanted.

"Please fill me," I whispered. "Please. I need to be filled with your cock. I want you to cum inside of me over and over again. I want you to give me everything you have."

He ran the back of his finger over my cheek, gently. My breath hitched, my nipples hardening. He leaned down again, his voice dark and soft.

"*More.*"

My voice trembled, my lips parting with a gasp as I felt part of his cock push inside of me. Just the tip, just enough to have every muscle in my body tensing.

"Please," I gasped. "Please, Alex. I need you to mate me. To breed me. I need you."

"More."

"Please," I cried, my hips jerking up.

He growled, giving me another inch.

"Alex," I groaned, my head tipping back. "Please!"

"She's begging so well for you Alex and you're being so mean."

Anne's words were a taunt. I groaned, turned on by the two of them. Alex only smirked, ignoring her.

"Do you want more, little spider?" he whispered.

"I'm begging you," I rasped.

"Good. Do you like being a good girl?"

"Yes," I said immediately.

It was true. I wanted to please him. I wanted to submit to him. I liked giving over the power, letting someone else take over for awhile.

And I really *really* liked being called a good girl.

"Oh," he whispered, his expression becoming almost feral. "Fuck. I like that look, baby girl."

I immediately moaned, his words sending a shiver through me.

"That one," he growled. "That one right there. Look at me like that while I give you my cock."

"Yes, Sir," I whispered.

He paused for a moment and then growled, his hips thrusting forward. I cried out as he filled me, giving me every inch. My pussy stretched around him, taking him completely.

"Good," he growled. "Fuck. You feel so fucking good, baby girl. You're doing so good for me."

Tears blurred my vision for a moment, the praise both turning me on and wrecking me.

"Don't cry," he whispered. "You're doing so good. No tears."

I tried to hold them back, letting out a sharp breath.

He wiped a single one away. "Remember your safeword."

"I will," I whispered. "It's not that. I just...It's intense to hear that."

He nodded, patient. So fucking patient. How had he ended up so sweet and patient while giving me a mind fuck and pussy fuck at the same time?

He pulled his hips back slowly before thrusting forward again, filling me. I cried out, my fingers digging into the blankets. I breathed in his scent, closing my eyes as I got lost to the shivers of pleasure building.

He began to move his hips faster, his cock driving in and out. He let out a possessive growl, his lips sucking on my nipple again.

I let out a soft scream as he bit down, the pain sending a whole different type of feeling through me.

I liked it. I more than liked it.

"Harder," I gasped. "Please. Please use me."

He groaned, his tongue swirling over the bite mark before he did it again. I felt his teeth sharpen, surprising me as he sank them in.

My upper back arched, a scream piercing the room as his teeth broke skin. He began to fuck me harder, sucking blood from the bite mark.

What kind of witch was he? The thought burned through me for a moment before disappearing, succumbing to him. Everything *him*.

I gave in completely, my legs wrapping around his hips as he drove into me. He growled, moving to my other breast and biting down. The pain and pleasure were a double-edged sword, driving me straight back to cumming.

I cried out, an orgasm bursting through me. My nails raked over his muscles, the primal urge to mate him making me groan.

I had to fight it. I felt my teeth lengthen, fangs emerging. Dripping with venom, desperate to take him. To tie him to me, to be his little spider forever and always.

"Do it," he whispered, grunting.

His body was hot, his cock still hard as he fucked me.

"Do it," he snarled.

"Are you sure?"

"Sylvia," he rasped. "I want you."

Fuck. It was all I needed to hear. He buried his cock in me to the hilt, crying out right as I leaned up and sank my fangs into his shoulder. I heard Anne's gasp of surprise, but it was drowned out by the pounding of his heart and the rush of his magic.

It burned. I felt the bond between us, one that was ancient. It *hurt*.

I pulled my fangs free with a gasp, staring up at him. I

sat up, moving back from him, shocked by the pain of the bond. Shocked by whatever this was.

Anne let out a hiss, moving to the bed. She glared at him, and even though we weren't bonded, I could feel her uneasiness.

"What *are* you?" I whispered, the pain bursting through me again.

I doubled over, letting out a gasp. I could feel our bond taking root, digging into my very soul.

Alex stared at us, his eyes even more luminescent. Blood wet his lips, and venom dripped from the bite I had just left.

I could feel *him*.

"Are you scared?" he whispered.

"No," I said, even though my heart was pounding.

Anne let out a hiss. "What the fuck is happening?"

Alex was silent and simply moved off the bed, standing at the end.

His cock was still hard even though his cum dripped from me. I could feel his heat now, our bond pouring his feelings into me.

"Alex," I whispered.

"You can't lie here," Anne snapped. "You can't lie to us. Not if we're to be your mates."

"Sylvia already is my mate," Alex said.

My lips parted, a pain tearing through my chest. Not because of his magic or the bond, but because his tone hurt.

Without another word, Alex left, slamming the bedroom door behind him.

"What the fuck," I whispered.

Anne let out a scathing growl. "I'm giving him about twenty minutes to work through whatever fucking tantrum this is, and then we're tying him up and getting some answers."

That wasn't usually my style, but I agreed.

Whatever had just happened— it felt like Alex and I had just built a wall between us instead of a bridge.

CHAPTER TEN
mistakes and mercy

ALEX

I WAS A MONSTER, MORE SO THAN ALFRED IN MANY ways. Seeing the look on Sylvia's face, her realization that I hide so much from everyone— it felt like my mask had just been ripped off.

She was upset. I could feel her, could feel that leaving her just now had hurt.

I was being self destructive again, and that realization had been why I had run.

Not that I could go far. Anne and Sylvia were in my bedroom, and I was standing outside on my porch, naked and still hard. There was a shield around my home to keep prying eyes away, so this wasn't the first time I'd been out here nude.

I should have been freezing standing here. It was fucking January and cold, but I simply couldn't feel anything except for the infernal burning of my heat.

I was a witch, this much was true. But, in my time, witches hadn't been what they were today. There weren't many left from the year I was born.

Time was strange, and I had grown very used to how quickly it moved. It didn't feel like it had been a few hundred years, but it had.

My body didn't show my age. There were times I was still an idiot too, and maybe this was one of them.

I was a witch, and I had originally been a weak one. Then, I had made deals. Deals with demons, with monsters.

Most of those deals had already been filled or finished. I had retained my power, growing and growing.

Then, I had summoned Aamon.

I had thought I could control him. I had believed he would be the demon I could get the most power from.

His price had been for me to let him use magic. We had created a blood pact, one that allowed me to continue to grow stronger, while allowing him to use magic.

Over the years, he had figured out how to harvest that magic from other witches. I hadn't even cared. I had turned a blind eye to everything, letting him do as he pleased, so long as I got what I wanted.

I was selfish.

Slowly, over the years, I had started to become more and more of a monster— while Aamon had become closer and closer to being a witch. The only thing was, we both needed the power of the other.

Then, something happened. My memory was still fuzzy around the event, but I had gone in search of a stone. One that was said to give magic power unlike anything else.

I had found it.

I destroyed it.

When I destroyed it, I had changed something. I had gotten too close to being like a monster. Too close to Aamon, too close to being something I shouldn't.

I went into heat.

Aamon had been there. He had been there, eating up my magic. Wanting me.

That's when things had started to change.

At first, I didn't notice. I didn't realize there were other witches who were omegas.

Aamon had been the one to figure that out.

The stone had given me power unlike any other, but at a cost.

My cock hardened and I let out a little gasp, looking up at the sky. My blood burned with heat, the taste of Sylvia on my lips.

I had just taken a mate and fucking dragged her into my life. I had punished her by letting her get close to me like this.

I hadn't been able to say no. The moment I saw her fangs, I had wanted her.

I wanted Anne too.

My chest ached. I had been waiting for so long. Going through so many heats, so many seasons unmated.

The door slid open behind me and I turned right as Anne grabbed me and yanked me inside.

I didn't get a word in before Sylvia shocked me. Webs burst from her fingertips, sticking to me.

"Hey!" I snapped.

Anne turned me around and Sylvia used her webs to tie my hands.

I struggled against them but it happened fast. Within

moments, I was bound like a fucking mummy and plopped on my couch.

Fuck.

"What the fuck?" I snarled.

Anne slammed the sliding door shut and came back to the couch, leaning over me. Sylvia sat down in one of the chairs, both sets of arms folded over her chest.

"Spill everything," Anne said.

I glared at her, but then I felt her hand close around my cock.

"Hey," I growled. "That's not fair."

Her touch sent a thrill through my entire body though. I fought off a groan, my fever returning completely.

She raised a brow. "Ask me to stop then."

I couldn't. I couldn't ask her to stop.

I growled, glaring at her. "Let me go."

She shook her head, the snakes around her face hissing at me. "You're being a dick. Tell us what is happening, Alex. You have been running from the truth for so long, hiding things from everyone at the office since all of this began. I want to know everything. And I want to know why the fuck you keep acting like this."

"Like what?" I hissed.

"Acting like the entire world revolves around you," she said. "There have been other people that have been hurt. And someone else was hurt tonight, by you. You didn't have to behave like that, in fact maybe if you tried being honest, you would find things would go a lot better for you. Instead, I had to drag you in from the cold, tie you up, and now you're hostage on your own couch."

"Oh is that right?" I growled. "Am I a hostage now?"

She started to stroke my cock, her eyes burning with both rage and mischief. "Yes," she whispered. "You're a hostage. I won't let you come until you decide to tell us the truth."

"Evil," I growled.

"No. What's evil is the fact that I was about to get off watching you and Sylvia, and then you decided to be a dick and ruined it all."

She started to stroke my cock faster, edging me. I let out a helpless moan, my hips bucking. I tried to push against my restraints, but Sylvia's webs were stronger than steel. Sylvia only let out a soft laugh, watching from her seat.

"You won't get out of those, *mate*."

Fuck. I knew I had fucked up, but now It was staring me in the face. My hips bucked, another groan leaving me.

"I'm sorry," I rasped. "I'm sorry Sylvia."

Anne laughed now. "Are you going to tell us now?"

Could I? Could I tell them everything?

My breath hitched, my cock throbbing. I was so close to cumming.

Anne pulled her hand away, her gaze locking with mine.

"Damn it," I whispered. "I don't want to tell you everything."

"Are you scared?" Sylvia asked, repeating what I had asked her earlier.

The answer was yes.

Yes, I was scared.

I was scared that I just found both of my mates, and that telling them everything would drive them away from me. What if they heard about all of the mistakes I had made and decided that they didn't want me anymore? I wouldn't blame them. How could I?

"Yes," I whispered. "I am scared."

"Tell us," Anne said softly. "We're here for you, even though you're an idiot."

I stared at the ceiling for a moment and then relaxed, my heartbeat finally slowing.

"Fine," I whispered. "I'll tell you everything."

CHAPTER ELEVEN
wednesday webs

ANNE

After everything Alex had shared with Sylvia and me last night, the three of us had ended up curling up in bed and sleeping.

Well, the two of them slept. I lay awake and stared at the popcorn on the ceiling, thinking about everything that had happened the last few months.

Alex had been a mystery through it all. He was good at evading questions, even better at telling lies. It made sense, given his age. I was uneasy about the fact that we had to force the truth out of him, but then again…

There was a weight that held him down that I couldn't understand. I had never reached so high only to fall so far. His hunger for power had destroyed so many lives, and he hated himself for it.

I knew other creatures like that. I hadn't lived as long as him, but I had known monsters in my life who had destroyed themselves on their quests.

Alfred would come back for him. Alfred was obsessed with power, but instead of turning away from it, he had held on to it with a death grip. I was certain he had already been evil, but Alex turning him away had made him even more so.

I understood obsession. I had seen what it could do to a monster.

What it could do to anyone for that matter.

I thought of my mother for a moment, her memory always a black hole of dread for me. Gorgons were infamous creatures, and our family in particular always lived with the haunting of my grandmother. It had never bothered me, but my mother? It had always been too much for her.

She had been like Alfred in a way. Hungry for something, willing to destroy others to get it. For her, it had been fame. To outshine her own mother.

It had never worked of course, and I had been the greatest disappointment. Especially when I had taken a job at an office with other creatures.

Warts and Claws had been good for me though. The last few months had been hell, but aside from that, I did love what we did. The app that creatures could use for dating had already helped many, and I hoped it would continue to merge the world of monsters and humans together.

Morning light started to filter into the room through the windows. Every minute that passed, the shapes of Alex's room became more apparent. I blinked, my thoughts still turning.

Alex was curled up between Sylvia and me, his body hot. I looked over at him, studying his expression.

He looked a lot younger when he was sleeping.

He stirred, a soft breath leaving him. I watched him wake up, enjoying it way too much.

Was that weird? Maybe, but I didn't care.

He had told us everything last night about Alfred. About his life. About him.

His eyes slowly opened, his bright blue irises reminding me of a storm. He blinked a few times, his brows drawing together.

His head turned and he looked over at me, his breath hitching.

"Morning," he whispered.

Fucking hell, he had a good morning voice.

"Morning," I said, sliding my hand over his chest.

He closed his eyes again, drawing in a long breath. He shivered beneath my touch as I moved my hand down to his cock, not surprised to find it hard.

"Fuck," he whispered. "*Anne.*"

"We never got to finish what we started," I murmured.

He nodded, his cheeks blooming with heat.

I sat up slowly, peeking at Sylvia. She was still fast asleep.

I gave a silent nod to the door and slid out of bed carefully, moving to the living room. I swept the snakes around my head up into a bun, securing them so he wouldn't get bit. Alex followed me, shutting the bedroom door behind him.

I turned right as he came to me, meeting him in a hungry kiss. He slid his hand behind the curve of my neck, devouring me. He pushed me against the back of the couch, his cock pressing against me.

"Alex," I groaned.

He kissed down my neck, every touch heated. I ran my fingers through his dark hair, gripping it as he lowered himself in front of me.

"I like it when you get on your knees for me," I whispered.

He looked up at me for a moment, letting out a sleepy chuckle. "You'd keep me here all day, wouldn't you?"

"I mean...what secretary doesn't dream about dominating their boss?" I teased.

His eyes flashed, a brow raising with challenge.

I was enjoying our dynamic more than I should have. Both of us were switches, which meant that our power struggle was fun.

"Make me cum and then fill me with your cock," I commanded.

"So demanding," he huffed, but he didn't disobey.

He slid his fingers over my slit, filling my opening with his tongue. I gasped, the touch sending a spear of need through me.

He gripped my hips, holding my pussy to his mouth. I groaned, my head falling back as he began to tease me. His tongue drove inside me, my pussy pulsing around him.

"Alex," I growled.

He pulled his tongue free for a moment, licking his lips. "Don't wake Sylvia up. She was sleeping hard."

I snorted, but I covered my mouth to hold back a cry as he drove his tongue back inside of me.

"Fuck," I whispered.

It wasn't fair how good he was at this. He ate me out like a dying witch, like I was the last thing he'd ever taste.

I stifled a growl and gripped his hair, thrusting my hips against him. My nipples hardened, my breaths coming faster as he drove me wild.

His fingertips dug into me harder as he continued, flicking his tongue over my clit. I gasped, swallowing a cry.

"Don't stop," I whispered. "I'm so close."

"Already? Did you think about me all night? You could have woken me up, little viper."

Fuck. I could feel my control slipping, his tongue alone stealing the reins.

His tongue flicked over my clit again and I gasped. He pushed two of his fingers inside of me, moving them as his tongue teased me. Driving me wild.

"Alex," I moaned.

He was relentless. I gave in to the pleasure that was washing over me, letting it drag me down. I leaned back against the couch, my tail curling around him. His cock was hard and dripping precum, his body so warm against the coolness of mine.

With a cry, I came hard— my eyes squeezing shut with ecstasy. He held my hips still as I shuddered around him, his tongue lapping up every drop of my essence.

He sat back on his haunches, looking up at me. "Good girl," he whispered.

I let out a helpless grunt, melting against him. He kissed up my body, rising up. I gasped as he pressed the head of his cock against my opening.

"You're so big," I groaned.

He grunted, taking my mouth again. Our tongues clashed together as he gave a hard thrust, filling me completely.

Our kiss broke as he groaned and I gasped, my muscles tensing as I adjusted around him.

"Gods," I rasped.

He growled, driving his cock even deeper. He held on to me, pulling his hips back before filling me all over again.

I cried out, wrapping my arms around his neck as he fucked me. I could feel him giving in to his heat, his movements becoming rougher and less polished.

"Harder," I gasped.

The couch scraped the floor as it moved, his thrusts becoming harder. I held on to him, his cock filling me over and over again.

I closed my eyes, fighting to stay quiet. To not scream out.

Mine. Alex was mine. I was so fucking sure of it now, could feel the word pumping through my veins.

My boss was my mate.

"Fuck," I huffed, pleasure stabbing through me.

Alex let out a sharp gasp, his fingers digging into me hard enough to leave marks. I could feel the hum of his magic, his body almost electric against mine.

"I love you," I gasped.

The words slipped out before I could stop them, swinging out of nowhere.

Alex didn't even skip a beat, driving into me harder. "I love you, too," he growled. "Fuck, I'm going to cum."

My thoughts were swirling as he gave one last thrust, his hot cum filling me with a groan. He panted, his chest rising and falling as his seed came inside of me.

We held on to each other, our breaths loud.

"Anne," he whispered, his voice breaking. "I do. I do love you."

"This is crazy," I murmured.

It was. But then again, everything in my life had always been. I was a monster, a creature, and I knew deep down that this witch belonged to me.

Alex groaned, slowly pulling his cock free. His cum dripped from me, rolling down my luminescent scales.

"Well. Good morning."

We both looked up to see Sylvia standing in the bedroom doorway, wearing a sleepy smirk.

Naked too.

My eyes roamed over her body, and I was already turned on again.

"How long have you been there?" I asked.

"Long enough to get a show," she said.

"We were trying not to wake you," Alex chuckled.

"No, it's okay, I think I like waking up to the sound of Anne moaning."

I grinned, my muscles relaxing. "How about you come clean up his mess then?"

"Only if I get rewarded."

"You will be," Alex said, taking a step back. "Come here, little spider."

Sylvia stood for a moment and then came to us. She was gorgeous, her long black hair swept behind her shoulders. The red mark on her chest was waiting to be licked, her nipples already hard.

Alex pulled her into a kiss, cupping her face gently for a moment before pushing her down to her knees in front of me. Sylvia licked her lips and I gasped as she kissed up to my slit, the tip of her tongue lapping up the drops of his cum.

"Mmm," she moaned. "You taste good."

"Good," Alex said, his voice husky.

His cock was already hard again, his hand falling down to it. He started to stroke himself, his cheeks flushed with heat.

I moved my tail around the two of them, tugging them closer to me. I reached for Alex as Sylvia ran her tongue around my pussy, taking his cock into my own hand.

He groaned, his hips bucking.

I had an idea, one that we'd had last night but never got to.

"Alex," I said, my voice soft and sultry. "Will you let us please you?"

"Yes," he said immediately.

Sylvia paused in cleaning up his cum, looking up at the two of us. She met my gaze and then smirked, knowing what I wanted to do.

In one swift motion, she had Alex pushed back against the living room wall. He gasped, not expecting her strength.

"Good girl," I said. "Use your webs."

Alex cursed as she pinned his arms above him, using her webs to hold them up. They bound his wrists to the wall, leaving him pinned and helpless.

His eyes darkened, but he didn't protest.

Sylvia turned to look at me, waiting for more instruction. I reached for her, pulling her into a kiss. The taste of Alex's cum filled both of our mouths, pleasure running through us.

She broke the kiss for a moment with a soft gasp, looking at him. "I can feel how much we turn you on," she said to Alex.

He nodded, his magic now humming around him.

"You do," he rasped. "I might have a monster kink."

"Oh yeah?" I asked. "Do you like it when your little viper and spider kiss?"

"Yes," he whispered hungrily, his eyes feasting on us.

"Maybe Sylvia will shift for us," I whispered, curling my fingers in her hair.

She groaned, her eyes pleading. "Fuck. Every time you touch me..."

"You love it," I said. "I like being in control sometimes."

Alex raised a brow, pulling against the webs. "Sometimes, huh?"

I smirked. "Yes. Sometimes. Little spider, keep him distracted. I'm going to suck his cock and see how long he can last before he cums again."

"I like a challenge," he growled, which only made me laugh.

He wasn't going to last more than five minutes between the two of us.

CHAPTER TWELVE
vipers and spiders

SYLVIA

Alex was trapped against the wall, his cock hard and dripping. His skin was flushed, his cheeks red and eyes bright blue.

I flicked the tip of my tongue over his nipple, listening to his immediate cry. He yanked against the webs, trying to pull free with a groan.

"Silly," I whispered. "You're trapped now. Helpless to your monster girls."

I could feel his surprise through our bond at my words.

I was surprised too, but I was enjoying this way more than I thought possible.

Last night had kind of been a train wreck, but after hearing about everything from Alex, I at least understood him more. Still, any of the feelings I had flew out the window the moment I heard Anne moaning in the living room this morning.

"Fuck," Alex growled. "Fuck, you're both just turning me into a slut."

I liked the idea of that.

Anne chuckled, her tail wrapping around Alex and me. She leaned down, her tongue swirling over the head of his cock.

Alex hissed, his muscles tensing.

I kissed up his chest, focusing on our bond. On teasing him. On making him become harder for Anne.

"Sylvia," he rasped.

I loved the way he said my name. I paused, sucking one of his nipples again before capturing his mouth. He moaned as we kissed, our tongues clashing.

He yanked against the silken ropes again, biting my bottom lip as he fought. I shoved him back, holding him still as Anne continued to tease his cock.

He broke the kiss, cursing. "Fuck. I *won't* cum."

"Liar," I breathed. "You will for us."

His eyes flashed and he yanked harder against the webs that bound him, only for his expression to change right as Anne took his cock all the way down her throat.

I loved submitting, but seeing him like this was also fun.

"Payback for last night," I said.

His eyes narrowed as he gasped. "Maybe I will spank you for saying that."

"Maybe," I giggled, circling his nipples with my fingertips. "But right now you can't."

"Fuck," he muttered. "Not you too."

Anne broke free from his cock for a moment with a laugh. "Serves you right. She'll be a brat before you know it."

Anything he was about to say died on his lips as Anne

took his cock back down her throat, sucking him. I looked down, watching as she pleased him.

Alex was helpless and so fucking close already.

"Cum for me," I whispered, holding his gaze.

His eyes widened, his breath hitching.

"Please," I said softly. "I just want you to cum. Please, Daddy."

Alex growled, his expression becoming feral. "Fucking hell. Say that again."

"Please, Daddy," I whispered. "Please. I want you to cum so badly. I want you to cum in her mouth so I can kiss her and taste you."

That's all it took. Alex almost looked angry as he let out a cry, his hips jerking as he started to cum again. I watched as Anne swallowed every drop until he was finally done, his body slumping against the wall.

Anne leaned back, licking her lips. "Someone has a Daddy kink."

"Me," I said, "it's me."

"And me," Alex rasped. "Fuck. Let me down so I can do more to both of you."

"No," Anne said. "I think you should stay there while we cook breakfast"

"Anne," Alex growled. "Let me down."

She rose up, dragging me close to steal a kiss. I tasted him between us, and that turned me on.

"Anne, so help me gods."

Anne grinned, breaking our kiss. "Should we leave him for a bit, my love? Let him think about what he wants to do to us."

I felt like I was a traitor in a way, but in a fun sort of way.

We both looked at him, his exasperation making Anne giggle.

"Just for breakfast," I said. "We'll make you some food and then you can punish us."

My eyes fell back down to his cock, where he was already getting harder again.

"I'm going to make you both regret this," he whispered.

"Oh I'm sure," Anne said. "Looking forward to it. Come on, Sylvia, let's make him some food and then maybe I will have a little breakfast of my own before we let him go."

I paused for a moment, feeling our bonds tighten... but it wasn't in a bad way. Anne grabbed my hand and tugged me towards the kitchen despite his protests.

"Good morning," she said, going to the coffee pot.

I giggled, leaning against the counter as she got it ready.

"I can literally hear both of you," Alex called.

I snorted. "This is fun. Although, honestly, I think I'm still half asleep."

"Mhm. We will wake you up properly. Some coffee and then maybe I can get a little taste of you..."

Her words sent a thrill through me. I nodded, watching as she made coffee and then opened up cabinets to find pans.

"Alex," she called. "Do you not have a big pan for eggs?"

"I'm not telling you!"

She cracked a fanged grin and kept searching until she finally fished one out.

"I can help —"

"No, sweetheart, you sit there and look pretty."

I blushed even though my tongue had literally just been inside of her and moved out of the way as she went to the fridge and pulled out breakfast items.

"Alex!"

I heard his sigh and poked my head around the corner, meeting his burning gaze.

"Where are the eggs?"

"I'm out!"

"For fuck's sake," Anne groaned. "Alright. Well, we'll have something."

"I can order some food," I offered.

"It'll be fine," she snickered. "I'm just giving him a hard time."

"Anne, I can literally hear you."

I fought another laugh this time, feeling Alex's frustration through the bond.

And horniness.

I reached into one of the cabinets and pulled down three coffee mugs. The scent filled the kitchen, the sound of the water percolating a comfort.

I wasn't even sure what time it was now, but morning light poured into Alex's house. It was a nice break from the gray skies that had been plaguing us for a couple months now.

I poured all of us a cup and then looked around, holding mine to my chest. The warmth felt good.

"You're too pretty," Anne said, pausing for a moment to look at me.

I smiled and leaned down, stealing a kiss from her. She let out a little moan and then gave me a pat. "You could go tease him if you want. Maybe give him some coffee."

"Maybe I should let him go," I said.

"No, not yet. Resist the urge," she hissed.

"Don't listen to Anne, Sylvia," Alex called.

We were both silent for a moment and then burst into laughter. I grabbed Alex's mug and carried ours to the living room, setting mine on the coffee table before going to him.

Alex was still bound to the wall, his cock still hard, and his head leaning against his bicep. His muscles were now highlighted from the morning sun, and he watched me come closer through a squint.

"Traitor," he whispered, but his lips tugged into a smile.

"You like it," I said. "I can feel it in our bond."

He relaxed some, his expression almost carefree. "You know what I feel in our bond?"

"What?" I asked, holding up his cup of coffee.

"Feed it to me," he whispered.

I hesitated for a moment, confused by what he meant. And then it clicked.

"You want me to spit your coffee in your mouth?"

"Yes," he said, still smirking.

"That's surely not what you feel in our bond," I said.

"No," he snorted. "I'll tell you after you give me coffee."

"What happened to you being Daddy?" I teased.

"Only good girls get Daddy," he answered. "Which.... If you let me go..."

"No," Anne hissed from the kitchen.

"Sorry," I said, taking a sip from his cup.

I held the hot liquid in my mouth and found myself rising up onto my tip toes. Alex parted his lips, his gaze locking with mine.

He was such a confusing man. One minute he had me begging to take his cock and the next he wanted me to spit hot coffee in his mouth.

Fuck.

Damned if both sides to him didn't turn me on though.

Mine. I could feel what he felt through our bonds, could feel how much he wanted me. How much I wanted him.

I did what he asked, spitting the coffee in his mouth. He swallowed, letting out a soft breath.

"Good girl," he whispered, his voice husky.

Fuck.

Oh.

I immediately felt my pussy throb, heat rolling over me. My breath hitched.

"Again," he whispered.

The control he had over me just by dropping his voice like that and calling me a good girl wasn't fair. Still, I took another sip and spit it into his mouth again.

His gaze never left me. It seared me, branding me as his.

I could feel our bond, the one we had so hastily made. I could feel his magic, his power, everything.

"Let me go," he breathed.

I paused for a moment, my heart hammering in my chest. I wanted to obey him, wanted to let him go and find out what he had in store for us.

His head leaned forward, his lips curving against my cheek.

"My love," he said, his voice husky. "Let me go so I can touch you. Please."

My breath shuddered and I looked back at the kitchen, damn near jumping out of my skin. Anne was watching us, her gaze pinned on me. She arched a brow and rolled her eyes.

"I'm almost finished with breakfast."

I smiled and then looked back at Alex. I leaned up and pulled the webs free, the silk always bending to my touch.

"Make it look so easy," Alex said, watching as the wisps fell to the floor.

I opened my mouth to respond, only to be picked up in one swift motion. I squealed as Alex thew me over his shoulder and carried me to the kitchen, holding me as he went to Anne.

"I just want you to know," Alex said, "I'm going to make you scream after we eat."

Anne laughed. "Good. I'd like that. Now, put our girlfriend down and get some plates and stuff. We're having some potatoes, sausage, and toast."

CHAPTER THIRTEEN
wolves at the door

ALEX

THE THREE OF US HAD BREAKFAST TOGETHER AND I WAS already making plans on how to punish both of them for tying me up, even though I had secretly liked it.

I'd like punishing them more though, that was for sure.

Anne raised a brow as she watched me finish the last of my food.

I swallowed hard, trying not to cave to my heat. Her and Sylvia were making that especially difficult though.

My cock was still hard. Again. Even after filling Anne earlier. I could feel my blood heating, my magic growing restless as I yearned more and more to breed both of them.

There was a part of me that couldn't believe the two of them were here. I didn't feel like I deserved to have two women who wanted me, and even through everything, the thought was haunting me.

I was scared I would hurt them, just like I had hurt everyone else.

I heard my phone go off and looked up, seeing it on the coffee table in the living room. I stood and snatched it up, the screen lighting up.

Unknown: I'm coming for you, Alex.

My stomach twisted, all of the breakfast I had just inhaled threatening to come right back up.

Unknown: I came back from hell just for you. You either come with me this time, or I will destroy Warts & Claws for good.

I stared at the texts, my thoughts spinning.

A soft voice echoed through the room, but I couldn't even hear it.

Alfred. Alfred truly was back and was hunting me. I was in heat. What if he knew?

The thought frightened me more than I cared to admit.

I was powerful. I had strong magic and was able to use the magic of others as well to aid me. Using everyone's magic, I was able to send him to hell.

It had just been a stroke of misfortune and perhaps fate that had broken him out again.

Unknown: I will kill your mates. I will kill your employees. You can't hide from me. Not anymore. I'm coming for you.

A shiver worked up my spine and for a moment, I swore I could feel his monstrous breath on the back of my neck.

"Alex!"

I snapped my head up, my eyes wide.

Anne and Sylvia were standing in front of me, both of them staring at me with concern.

"What is it?" Anne whispered, her eyes darting to my phone.

I couldn't lie to them.

I took a deep breath and released it, steeling my nerves. "Alfred," I whispered. "He texted me."

"Fuck," Anne hissed.

Sylvia paled, her eyes immediately becoming distant. I could feel the strike of fear run through her.

I hated that.

I didn't want her to be scared.

One of her hands rested on my arm and I took one of the others, giving her a soft reassuring squeeze.

I handed Anne my phone, letting her read for herself what the bastard had said. She let out a frustrated hiss, glaring down at the texts. Her diamond pupils grew bigger, the snakes around her head hissing too.

"I wonder if he knows," she said, scowling. "Does he know where you live? Has he ever been here before?"

"Not that I am aware of," I said. "I moved after they kidnapped me last. I did my best to make sure no one found out, but he is difficult to hide from."

"Fuck," Anne cursed again. "You need to let Inferna know. We should video call her."

"We should put clothes on first then," Sylvia said, letting go of my arm. "I'll go grab them."

Anne and I watched as she went to my bedroom. Sylvia shut the door too, putting space between us.

"Anne," I said under my breath. "I want both of you to go to safety."

"And leave you alone and in heat?" she snapped. "No."

"I will be okay," I said, even though the idea of being alone right now felt like torture.

"No," she said again. "No. I won't leave you, Alex. You're not alone."

"He will hurt everyone—"

"I said no!" she shouted, the snakes around her head roaring to life.

She hissed at me, her fangs dripping with venom. I wasn't scared of her, but the outburst did make me freeze.

Her tail wrapped around me and she pulled me close to her, her hand sliding up and curling into my hair. She held me tight, our gazes burning into each other.

I had been working with her for months, and knew that when she said no, she would fight tooth and claw for it.

"Alex," she whispered. "You can't push me away. You can't push her away. You belong with us, and we will defeat him together. You've already sent him to hell once before. We can do it again."

"He will change tactics," I growled. "He will use my ability to do so to his advantage. This monster is just playing a game with us, Anne, and he wanted to be the king."

I couldn't let him take her or Sylvia from me.

His texts burned in my mind, my heart beating faster.

Did he know where I lived?

Had I led him straight here?

He said he'd kill my mates which meant he knew about Anne and Sylvia.

Did that mean he knew about my heat?

All of the questions filled my mind, driving me crazy. I couldn't stand the thought of him hurting my mates. I had been waiting so long for them.

"He won't win," she said, shaking her head. "He won't. I swear it. I won't let him. I have seen everyone else in this fucking office get their happy ending and gods damn it. I want mine, Alex. I want you. I want Sylvia. I want the three of us to be able to find some happiness in this fucked up world. Is that too much to ask for?"

"No," I whispered. "No, it's not. But we won't get that

until he is dead. And we won't get that if you or Sylvia or anyone else is dead either."

"He won't touch her," she snarled. "Never again. I don't know exactly what happened while she was trapped, but I would personally like to drive a fucking stake through his heart."

Her passion made me take a deep breath, bringing a little smile to my lips. I leaned forward despite the hissing snakes and stole a kiss, enjoying the taste of her. The feel of her.

She relaxed until she pulled away, and then leaned her head on my chest.

"It'll be okay, little viper," I whispered.

Would it be?

Sylvia came back in the room with clothing in three of her arms, her expression unreadable. She let out a sigh as she handed me a set and then Anne too, and then swept her long black hair back over her shoulders.

Anne and I broke apart and the three of us got dressed, silence settling over us. We were all deep in thought.

"One meeting and then I'm tearing these off," I said.

"Agreed," Sylvia chuckled, pulling on a shirt.

My eyes fell to her breasts and I watched, sadly, as she covered them. She rolled all of her eyes. "Such a horny witch."

"I am," I said, smiling even though I was still worried.

Within a couple of minutes, the three of us were taking seats on the couch. I had grabbed my laptop and set it up, hitting the call button to Inferna.

It immediately picked up, and I wasn't surprised to see Art and Calen sitting with her in a conference room.

"Well, well," Art teased.

I rolled my eyes, but didn't fight my smile.

"Good morning," I said.

"Morning," Inferna said, arching a brow.

Fuck. I loved working with her but her knowing smirk made me want to slam the laptop closed.

"Alfred just texted me," I said, getting straight to it.

"He texted me too," Inferna said, pressing her lips into a thin line. She shook her head, grimacing. "I will personally be giving my uncle hell. For all of us."

"Please do," Anne hissed.

"What did your texts say?" I asked.

"What you would expect," Inferna sighed. "We're all going to die, Warts and Claws will end. Our loves will perish unless we deliver you with a little bow on your head to him."

"He wanted a bow?" I scoffed.

"No, that was sarcasm, Alex," Inferna said bluntly.

"Still."

I skipped a beat for a moment, taking a breath. Sarcasm went over my head a lot, and I blamed it on my age. "Mine basically said the same thing. He's coming for me."

"I think it would be good to move you," Inferna said. "I can call my family. Hell, maybe you can stay with Lucifer."

"No," I said. "I don't want others brought into this. But, I do think everyone should take the rest of the week off. Get out of the city even. I'll pay for that, I don't care. I just want everyone to get to safety."

"No," Inferna said. "Everyone has refused to leave."

"What do you mean?" I asked.

"I already thought of this," she said, shrugging. "I offered to give everyone time off, to send everyone away. And every single witch and monster who has been involved in this declined. They will be here to help if needed, and stated that they would rather send Alfred back to hell than leave you alone."

I was silent, her words settling in. I leaned back, not sure what to say.

Why would any of them be willing to help me? All of this was my fault. All of the danger, the pain, the suffering.

"Like it or not," Inferna said, "you were responsible for some of this, but not all of this, Alex. You are a victim too. And like it or not, you are also part of the reason why I met my mates. Why the others met theirs. There has been good that has come out of this situation, not just bad, and quite frankly— not a single one of us would change how things have happened. I know that you want us gone, but we won't leave."

Tears blurred my vision and I was still at a loss for words.

"I don't deserve that," I whispered.

"Sure you do," Inferna said. "Of course you do. For fuck's sake. Do you really think we'd just let him take you?"

Anne's hand gripped my thigh, giving me a gentle squeeze.

"No," Anne said, looking at me. "We won't. That won't happen."

"I just... he will go for Anne and Sylvia," I said, looking from one to the other. "I don't want either one of you to get hurt."

"We might get hurt," Sylvia said, shrugging. "But this isn't my first time, Alex, and I have a reason not to let him win. I won't give in like I did last time."

"We will win," Inferna said. "I am sure we will. His time is coming to an end all over again. But first, I need the three of you to go somewhere unless you are sure you aren't being watched."

"I will have to look," I said, glancing at the windows. I felt a bolt of paranoia, but it was warranted.

Was the wolf already at my door or did we have more time?

Inferna nodded, leaning forward. "Let us know. Maybe have some sex first because you look like you're running a fever."

"Inferna," I hissed.

She laughed, shrugging. "I'm an incubus and the boss."

"Not mine," I muttered.

"Sure, whatever you say Alex," she teased. "Let us know about that, and we will make a plan."

She always had a plan.

I sighed and nodded. "Fine. But, if it's too dangerous, I want everyone gone."

She made a face, the one that told me no one was going to listen to me. I narrowed my eyes.

"Inferna," I growled.

"Have fun," Inferna said, waving. "Anne, make sure to let me know."

"Will do," Anne said.

Before I could protest, Anne leaned forward and closed the call, then snapped the laptop shut.

"She's something else," I mumbled.

"She's right," Sylvia said, shrugging. "I can see why everyone wants to work for her."

It was true. Hell, I was her boss, and most days it felt like I worked for her.

One of Sylvia's hands slid over my thigh and then grazed over my cock. I let out a moan, my head falling back.

"Fuck. I can't think with both of you around," I sighed.

"Mhmm," Anne said, smirking. "It must be so hard to think when all your blood is in your cock."

I looked over at her, glaring. "Breakfast is over, little viper."

"And?"

I leaned forward, my voice dropping dangerously low. "Get on your fucking knees, or your punishment really won't be fun."

"I don't have knees." She smirked like she had already won.

"You have to the count of three, Anne, or so help me gods."

CHAPTER FOURTEEN
brat tamer

ANNE

I was in the mood to fuck around and find out.

Being a brat was apparently my new full time job, and I was taking that seriously.

Alex's eyes burned with a bit of anger, his glare making my heart pound.

"Three," he said.

For a moment there was silence, but then I felt the magic.

I gasped as he raised a hand, light bursting from his fingertips. My muscles immediately stiffened, everything going still. Even my snakes froze.

Alex stood up, looking at Sylvia. "I want you to sit in one of the chairs and watch like a good girl. And I want you to touch yourself while you do. Do you understand?"

The energy in the room sent a thrill up my spine, a mixture of dark controlling energy and desire.

"Yes, Daddy," Sylvia whispered.

Her submission turned me on, but it also made me nervous.

Sylvia went to one of the other chairs in the living room, her six eyes watching as Alex turned to look down at me.

He raised a brow. His magic came off him in waves, followed by the addictive scent of his heat.

I wanted to devour him. To drive him crazy, to crack him open and steal his heart.

These were monstrous thoughts, but I couldn't fight them.

Not when he was looking at me like he wanted to do the same thing.

"Such a bad girl," he whispered, reaching forward.

He lifted my chin, his lips tugging into a cruel smile.

I couldn't speak. Couldn't move.

I couldn't escape him.

He chuckled and let go of my chin, leaving my view.

"I'll be back. I have something I want to try on you. And remember, little spider," he said, looking at Sylvia. "Don't stop."

He disappeared for a few moments. I listened as he went to his bedroom.

Sylvia's gasp drew my attention, my eyes refocusing on her. She was touching herself, her thighs spread wide as she dipped her fingers into her wet pussy. It glistened, her essence coating her fingers.

Fuck. I could feel my own pussy throb in response. I wanted to lick her fingers clean, to get a taste.

Instead, Alex had me bound with his magic.

The restraint would drive me insane.

I heard him come back into the room, his footsteps light on the floor. He came around, carrying a couple of items with him that I hadn't expected to see.

Fuck. I was fucked.

Alex arched a brow, his expression devious.

Right now, in this moment, I understood why he was the boss.

I understood why he was in control.

I could feel my pussy throbbing. He reached forward, taking my jaw in his hand again.

"Do you consent to letting me take control? To using your safeword if needed? You may speak."

I could feel my throat soften, his magic letting me speak.

"Yes," I whispered.

"Good girl. Do you consent to letting me spank you? To letting me gag you?"

"Yes," I breathed.

"Good girl," he praised, stroking my cheek softly. "So good," he crooned. "Except when you're being a fucking brat."

I could still move my eyes. I squeezed them shut for a moment, wishing I could fight against the bonds. I wanted to push his buttons, to see just how harsh he could be.

"Try and make me submit," I whispered, my eyes flying back open. "I will never give in to you."

A low growl left him, one that sent a chill through me.

"We shall see, little viper," he said, still stroking my face. "You're so helpless right now. Bound by my magic. You only move because I allow you to. You're nothing but my fuck doll right now."

Fuck. His words made my breath hitch and my cunt drip.

He ran the pad of his thumb over my bottom lip, opening my mouth. He pricked his finger on my fang, the blood welling.

He smirked, holding it to his own mouth. He licked it up, his eyes searing me.

His gaze was a brand, and I could feel the fiery burn on my soul.

He left my mouth wide open, his chuckle making my heart beat faster. He turned to look at Sylvia, arching a brow.

"Where did your panties go, sweet girl?"

"On the floor," she rasped.

I could smell her arousal. She had been touching herself, teasing herself, getting ready to be fucked.

I wanted to fuck her.

"Let me go," I growled.

"No," Alex said, waving off my words. He leaned down and picked up Sylvia's panties, holding the black lace to his lips. "You said you wanted to drop these off for me the other night but never did."

"You're right," I said, my tone harsher than I intended.

Fuck, I was getting off on being a little bit mean.

Maybe there was something wrong with me, but I didn't give a fuck.

"I didn't think you deserved them," I whispered. "Just a stupid witch in heat."

"This stupid witch is going to make you scream, little viper."

"Scream, but it won't be your name."

He laughed now, one that was almost evil as he came back to me. He stuffed Sylvia's lace panties in my mouth, gagging me with them.

"We'll see, love. While you can't speak, if you need to stop, you will make a signal with your hands. You will be able to move them now."

I felt his magic lift, allowing just my hands and fingers to move.

"Show me the signal."

I did, showing him what I would make if I needed this to stop.

I didn't want it to.

I wanted him to do his worst.

My breathing was more ragged now, the taste of Sylvia's pussy filling my mouth.

"Our girl was wet," he whispered, winking at me.

Fuck.

Alex reached down and picked up an item he had set down on the couch.

I didn't know I liked being degraded like this.

I didn't know how much I liked to fight him.

There was a volatile energy between us, and I was on the losing side, but still...

I moved my hand and fingers, flipping him off.

Alex lifted a knife, one that had an engraved ivory handle and a blade that glowed blue like his magic. He held the tip to my cheek, and even though I couldn't move, I could feel the sting of it pressing against me.

I was instantly turned on even more, and so was Sylvia. I heard her breath hitch, her moan drifting through the room.

"You like pushing me," Alex whispered.

If I could say fuck you with my eyes, I would have, but even so— he got the message.

He dragged the blade down my face, careful not to actually cut me.

My heart was pounding wildly now, my palms pooling with sweat. I was excited and nervous.

"It would be a shame if my hand slipped," he whispered. "I would hate to leave a mark on you, little viper. And all because you don't know how to obey."

I dragged in a breath, her underwear making it harder to.

He chuckled, bringing the blade down the curve of my neck, over my collar bone, down to my breasts. I felt the tip of the knife circle one of my nipples, pressing a little harder this time.

A moan left me involuntarily.

I felt his free hand glide over my scaled hips, his fingers running over my slit.

My eyes fluttered, my breaths quickening.

I was so turned on but there was nothing I could do. I needed to cum so badly, was desperate to release.

"Aw baby," he crooned, pressing two of his fingers inside of me the same moment he pressed the knife against my nipple.

I cried out, but not because of the pain.

The pleasure was more excruciating than the pain.

He pulled his fingers free, holding them to his lips.

"By the time I'm done with you, you're going to be begging for our mating bond," he whispered.

I grunted, glaring at him even though I wanted that so fucking badly.

I wanted that bond.

I wanted one with Sylvia too.

The primal part of me, the monster part of me. The one that craved to be taken and mated and bred— all of it came together, warring against me.

I wanted to submit to him, but not until he at least broke a sweat trying to make me do so.

He licked his fingers and sighed, running the tip of the knife down my body.

I gasped as it went over my navel and then my scales, all the way down to my slit.

Now, I fought against the bonds. I fought against them hard, but it was no use.

Alex leaned forward and whispered in my ear as I felt the blunt end of the knife handle press against my opening. "You'd let me fuck you with this knife, wouldn't you?"

"*Fuhyu*," I snarled through Sylvia's panties.

He chuckled, pulling it back.

I was throbbing. I was dripping. I was hot and needy and desperate but I would not fucking show it.

"I can feel you," he whispered. "I can feel your lust. I can feel our connection even though we haven't made a bond yet. My magic loves you. I want to wrap you in it forever, little viper."

I had known that he could be dominant.

I had known that he could top me.

But I hadn't expect *this*.

I felt the handle of the knife push into my slit, filling me. I gasped, only for him to reach up and pinch my nose shut.

Fuck. *Fuck, fuck, fuck.*

For a moment, I thought about using my safeword. For a moment, I wondered if we were going too far.

But I wanted this.

I wanted him to break me.

I wanted him to control my breath, to control my orgasms.

He let go, allowing me to drag in a breath right as he gave me more of the handle.

A sharp breath left me, followed by him pulling it out and driving it back in like a cock.

I could feel the magic thrumming from it, could feel his power washing over me in waves.

Alex reached up and pulled the lace free, allowing me to breathe fully. I also felt the magic loosen around my head, allowing me to let it fall forward.

"Fuck you," I hissed. "Fuck you so much."

"Oops," he chuckled. "Back in time out, sweetheart."

I snarled, but he yanked my head back upright and the magic held me still. He grabbed the lace and shoved it in my mouth again, smirking like a god damned king.

I was furious now, but still turned on.

What a fucking bastard.

"Sylvia," Alex said, pulling the hilt of the knife free.

I groaned, wishing it would be replaced with his cock.

He tossed it to the side and turned, going over to her.

"Let's show her what good girls get as a reward, shall we?"

"Yes, Daddy," she rasped.

Alex leaned down, stealing a deep kiss from her. She groaned, one set of arms wrapping around his neck while her other hands continued to play with her pussy.

Fuck, I wanted four arms.

Alex lifted her, taking a seat in the chair and putting her on top of his lap. She gasped, holding on to him as his hand slipped between her thighs.

"Are you my good girl?"

"Yes," she gasped.

"Yes, Daddy."

"Yes, Daddy," she moaned, her head falling back.

"Good girls get orgasms, don't they?"

"Yes," she cried.

Her voice was already on edge, her muscles wound tight. I wanted to glare at him, but it was impossible with her in his arms— especially when she was moaning like that.

Alex slid his fingers inside of her and she cried out, her moans driving me wild.

Fuck. I fought hard against his magic again but it was to no avail. I dragged in more air, the taste of her pussy sweet.

I was desperate for the real thing though.

I mentally called Alex every bad name in the book, but it all ended in a spiral of need.

"Cum for me," Alex growled.

Sylvia cried out, her body arching as she came for him. It was glorious, her voice music to my ears.

She shuddered in his lap, her muscles relaxing. Alex held her tight, his eyes lifting to fall on me.

A challenge.

I held his gaze. I held it for as long as I could, until he finally asked me again.

"Do you want to be a good girl for Daddy?"

I felt the magic unravel, allowing my head to move.

I was still for a moment, but then I nodded.

"Sylvia," he said softly. "Do you think I should let her go?"

"Yes," Sylvia breathed. "Please fuck her. I want to watch. Please."

Her *please* was too damn sweet for such a demand.

Alex smirked and lifted her again, putting her back in the chair before he came to me.

I wanted him.

I wanted the bond.

I wanted to be his mate.

He pulled the lace free and planted a kiss on my lips.

I accepted it, our tongues intertwining.

I moaned as he slid his hand behind my neck, the magic releasing my entire body. I melted against him, my will finally crumbling.

He growled and swiped any items from the couch, laying me down on it. I groaned as he climbed on top of me, his cock hard as he kissed up my body.

"Mate me," I rasped. "Please."

"Not yet," he whispered.

"I'll be good," I cried.

He groaned, grinding his cock against my scales.

"Are you certain?"

I would be good.

For now.

"Yes," I whispered.

He chuckled now, knowing what that meant. "Good," he said, stealing another kiss from me.

I felt the tip of his cock press against my entrance. I was so fucking wet and in one swift motion, he filled me completely.

I groaned, arching against him. He held me close as his hips began to thrust, filling me with his cock.

"Alex," I gasped. "You feel so fucking good."

"Good," he groaned.

His breath hitched, his control slipping as he began to fuck me harder. I held on to him, my body responding to his touch. Pleasure ran through me, every stroke sending me closer and closer to the edge.

I was already so wet from everything that had happened, so fucking close to cumming.

I wanted him to fill me with his seed. I wanted it to drip from me.

Alex grunted, his hands grabbing my wrists and pinning them above my head.

"Mate me," he rasped.

I didn't wait for him to ask twice.

With a hiss, I leaned up and buried my fangs straight into his neck.

He whispered the spell, and I felt our mated bonds come to life.

I groaned right as an orgasm crashed into me at the same time, giving me a kind of ecstasy I'd never experienced in my life.

Alex cried out and I felt his cum fill me, his hot seed spilling inside of me.

I pulled my fangs free, the two of us melting together.

"I love you," I whispered.

"I love you too," he said softly. "So much."

CHAPTER FIFTEEN
confessions

SYLVIA

After the three of us had been fully satisfied, we'd thrown on some clothes and gone outside to see if there were any signs of Alfred. There had been none, which had been both alarming and comforting.

We'd come back inside, let Inferna know that there were no signs of him, and then we all agreed that a shower would be good.

It was to my delight that Alex had a very nice shower and a large bathtub in the bathroom that joined his room. The three of us rinsed off, and then Alex ran a hot bath with Epsom salts for us.

Anne opted to sit next to us on a soft stool as she didn't want to deal with her tail in the water, which meant I had a great view of her lounging, naked and gorgeous. Her scales shimmered, her skin smooth.

I looked away, blushing.

Both of my mates were hot.

I wanted to make a bond with her soon too.

Alex sighed happily, relaxing more. I smiled to myself, the heat of the water relaxing my muscles.

"I can almost forget about work," Alex chuckled.

"I *had* forgotten," Anne laughed.

I snorted, rolling my eyes. "I'd like to start work. It's been a strange time."

They both looked at me, and I could feel the curiosity.

I sighed, sinking down more into the tub. I knew that both of them wanted to know more about what had happened to me when Alfred had me trapped.

It had been a dark time. Literally and figuratively.

And then Ember happened.

I thought about my friend for a moment. She and her partners had become close to me, and so had Cinder and their partners. I had ended up with a little network of people I could rely on, that were there to help me figure out how to get my life back.

When I had disappeared there had been so many things that had gone wrong, and the world had assumed I was dead. Getting my bank account back had been step one, and there had been some magic involved to keep humans from asking too many questions.

"You can ask," I said.

"I don't want to pry," Anne said.

"Of course you do," I chuckled. "And that's okay. I can talk about everything now just fine."

Alex held his breath next to me for a moment and then let it out, cocking his head. "How did you end up trapped?"

"Well, I used to work at another branch of offices, one that Alfred had more control over. I was a manager like Inferna and eventually drew his attention. Slowly but surely, I started taking on extra projects for him until I realized it was hurting witches and monsters. Then, I tried to tell another manager, someone I thought I could trust. He turned out to be working with Alfred closely, so it was seen as a betrayal. I don't know how long I was held in the dark. The most monstrous part of me took over to survive, and well...I can live for a long time."

"I'm so sorry," Anne whispered.

I shrugged. I had come to terms with it and was thankful to be free. But, I would most likely never want to be completely in the dark again.

"It sucked," I said. "But I'm out of it and doing much better now."

Alex was silent, his eyes never leaving me. "I'm going to send him back to hell."

"Good. Because if you don't, I will," I said, sitting up straight. "I've been lucky. Lucky to have met Ember and everyone else here. And...everything that has happened between the three of us this week has been good too. I swore up and down I would never be involved with a witch though," I said, giving Alex a hard look. "Specifically an *omega*."

"We're kind of hard to avoid when fate says its time," he chuckled, beaming at me. "I can't complain. I've been waiting a very long time for the two of you."

I smiled at him, his words sending warmth through my chest.

Alex's eyes fell down to my breasts and I snorted, sending a splash of water towards him. "Eyes up here, mister."

He grinned, the tension breaking. "Between the two of you, it's difficult."

"Oh yes," Anne chuckled. "You must be so *hard*... I mean, it's so hard."

I could feel him respond to that, and it made me smirk. I looked at him, enjoying the way the flush crept over his skin.

"So difficult," Anne teased.

"Do you want me to tame you again, little viper? Didn't you agree to behave?"

"I don't remember that," she teased, looking over at him with a wink.

Alex rolled his eyes, but he relaxed again.

Lust crept over me, sneaking through my body. I looked between the two of them again, thinking about how I had watched them earlier.

It had been so fucking hot.

I wanted to watch them again.

Hell, I wanted to be between the two of them again.

Alex moaned softly. "Sylvia, I can feel you through the bond, little spider. Come here."

I obeyed him, moving across the tub. He pulled me into his lap, the hot water splashing around us. His cock was hard against my lower back, his arms wrapping around my waist.

Anne was watching us, her lips pulled into a sensuous smile.

Alex kissed my shoulder, sucking on my skin to leave a mark. I let out a gentle growl, my pussy throbbing.

His hand slid down my thigh, dipping between them. I gasped, leaning back against his chest. My head fell back on his shoulder, pleasure wringing me.

"Alex," I moaned. "Fucking hell."

Anne groaned and moved off the stool, moving around to the side of the tub. Alex turned me around so that I was straddling him, and so that Anne could pull me into a heated kiss while he sucked on one of my nipples.

I immediately cried out, the feeling intensifying as he sucked harder.

Anne's tongue danced with mine, her hands cupping my face. I reached down as we kissed, taking Alex's cock into my palm. He let go of my nipple for a moment to groan, his hips thrusting up.

"Fuck," he growled.

"Come to the bed," Anne said. "I have an idea I want to try."

"Yes, please," I said, curious about what she had in mind.

Anne paused for a moment, looking over at Alex. "Do you want to try too, *Sir?*"

Alex hissed between his teeth. "I swear," he chuckled. "Yes, I do."

She snickered as Alex lifted me. Water splashed onto the floor, but he snapped his fingers. The air sizzled with magic, the water going back into the tub.

He lifted me with ease, his muscles rippling as Anne led us back to the bedroom.

My head was spinning, my pussy pulsing. I wanted both of them so much. His scent was driving me insane, making my desire insatiable.

Alex set me down and then Anne pushed him back onto the bed. Alex raised a brow, propping his torso up so he could watch her.

"I'm very flexible," Anne said, her tail curling around me.

She moved, turning so that her back was facing him. I raised a brow, watching her with excitement. Her scales glittered, stray drops of water reflecting like diamonds. I watched as she started to lean back, bending so that her spine curled. She planted her hands to either side of Alex's hips, her body contorted into a back bend to that her lips were now hovering over our mate's hard cock.

"Oh," I whispered, her idea sending a thrill through me.

Alex let out a dark groan, his eyes fixated on her.

Her tail gave me a gentle tug and I stepped closer, her pussy now at the perfect angle for me to feast on.

"Fuck," Alex growled. "I do like this idea."

"So do I," I said, staring at her with wonder. "Are you sure you're comfortable?"

Anne answered that by taking the head of Alex's cock between her lips, moving so that she took more down her throat.

His head fell back, his eyes rolling with a moan. He cursed in a language I didn't know, one that sent sparks of energy through his bedroom.

I leaned forward, running my tongue over her slit. She moaned as she sucked his cock, her tail tightening around me. The tapered end spread my thighs, rubbing over my pussy as I drove my tongue inside of her. The taste of her was perfect.

I gripped her hips, groaning as I pushed my tongue farther before flicking it over her clit. The sound echoed through the room, followed by the sound of Anne sucking him.

Alex growled, followed by a moan. "Fuck, this is hot," he gasped.

I looked up, seeing the curve of her stomach and ribs, the soft mounds of her breasts. Her nipples were hard, her gorgon body perfect for this type of acrobatic position.

I could feel Alex's pleasure through our bond, and I could even feel hers through him too.

I craved a connection with her, wanted to feel her excitement as intimately as I felt his.

I ran my hands up her body while my others held her close. I had never complained about having four arms and hands, but especially in moments like this-- they came in handy.

Alex thrusted up, deep throating her hard. I held on to her, sucking on her clit as she took him.

She pulled up for a moment, breathing hard. I kept her from falling back, holding on to her as I continued.

"Fuck," she moaned. "You're making it so hard to concentrate," she gasped.

"Good," Alex said gruffly. "Take my cock again, little viper."

"Only because it feels good," she teased.

She then groaned, bending back.

I smiled against her, pausing for a moment to peek around and watch as she took his cock. I loved his gasp and the way I could feel him through our bond.

"Keep eating her out," Alex gasped.

"Okay," I said, smirking.

Anne's tail continued to play with me, the tip threatening to spear me. My head fell back for a moment, pleasure curling through me.

"You can fuck me with it," I gasped. "Please."

Anne growled, the tip of her tail thrusting inside of me. I cried out, my entire body tensing before relaxing.

I gasped, leaning forward again to drive my tongue inside her.

The three of us groaned together, the room echoing with our sounds of pleasure. Her tail filled me, thrusting in and out as I did the same to her pussy with my tongue, and Alex did the same to her throat with his cock.

"Good girls," he gasped.

He shuddered, his breath hitching.

"Fuck, I'm going to cum," he moaned.

"I'm close too," I gasped.

It was true. Anne's tail was driving me crazy, and the buzz of Alex's magic was starting to send me closer and closer to the edge.

The echo through our bonds was something I had never expected to turn me on so much, but it was as if our pleasure was feeding off each other.

Anne made a moan, a warning sound that she would soon be coming too. Alex grunted, thrusting up harder, his head falling back.

"Fuck," he growled.

"Cum," I gasped. "Please, Daddy."

I could feel that immediately make him almost cum.

I gave in to everything. To the electricity running through me, to the way Anne tasted, to the way her tail felt fucking me. All I could think about was cumming on her tail, and tasting her as she came too.

Alex cried out at the same time I did, our orgasms crashing into us simultaneously. I gasped, my entire body taking the wave of euphoria.

Anne lifted off his cock with a groan, sitting up and swallowing hard. I leaned up, catching the drop of his cum that dripped from her soft lips. She kissed me, holding on to me as I pushed two of my fingers inside of her and began to fuck her with them.

Her hands gripped my shoulders and she cried out, letting out a string of curses.

Alex sat up, his arms sliding around her. They cupped her breasts, pinching her nipples.

Our gorgon mate was now trapped between us, the two

of us doing everything we could to make her cum. Within a few seconds, she let out another sharp cry, her orgasm crashing into her.

Her chest heaved with breaths, her body melting between us. I pressed my forehead against her chest, breathing hard. My brain felt like it had been melted, my muscles turned to mush.

The three of us collapsed into the blankets, the ones that made up Alex's nest. I curled up next to him, sliding my hand up his chest to meet Anne's.

"I could sleep again," Anne sighed.

"Me too," I mumbled.

Every time I came hard, it felt like I was sent to another planet. The feeling lingered, everything feeling good.

I loved both of them so much. To think that earlier this week I had no idea any of this would happen... that I would meet two mates. I swallowed hard, thinking about how long I had wanted something like this.

All of my time in the dark, I had held on to the thought that I would escape. That I would have a life again. That I would be able to find someone. I had held on to the belief that I would escape and be swept off into the arms of someone who loved me.

It had kept me from losing myself to Alfred and his evil. It had kept me from dying.

Even so, I never thought I would be here.

I didn't want to be anywhere else.

Alex's fingers grazed over my skin, his hand settling on me while his other settled on Anne. I looked up at her, enjoying the fact that her cheeks were a little rosy. She smirked, giving me a loving look.

"I want to mate with you," Anne whispered, her hand gripping mine. "Not right this very second, but soon."

"Yes, please," I said, smiling against Alex.

"I volunteer to watch," he said.

I snorted, grinning again. I closed my eyes, taking a deep breath before relaxing again.

"I think it's nap time then."

CHAPTER SIXTEEN
thursday threats

ALEX

It was the middle of the night when I slipped out of bed and went to the living room. Anne was actually asleep, to my surprise, and so was Sylvia.

Earlier, the three of us had woken from our nap and had dinner before crawling back into bed for a movie and snuggling. Even between the two of them, I hadn't been able to fall asleep though.

It wasn't the heat that was keeping me awake, it was the thought that the three of us were being stalked by Alfred. He was very much alive, and while we hadn't been able to sense him anywhere close to my home, it made me nervous.

We'd try to switch places later today, but even that felt like a bad idea.

He was closing in. If it were any other person in the world, I might have told myself I was being paranoid.

But not with Alfred.

His texts had been clear yesterday.

He was coming for us.

I was freshly mated now, still in heat, although it was starting to lessen since Anne and I had made our bond. I could feel both of them now, and it grounded me.

But, it also made me scared. It made me scared that he would take them away from me.

I still didn't like that everyone refused to leave too. I didn't want anyone else to get hurt.

It was a clusterfuck all over again.

I drew in a deep breath and went to the kitchen, wandering to the fridge. I started to reach for the fridge, but then paused.

A chill worked over me. A warning.

I felt my magic react, my fingertips buzzing.

I looked back into the darkness of the living room, narrowing my eyes.

I wasn't alone.

Somehow, someone had slipped in.

Fuck.

The thought enraged me to a point that nearly tipped me into seeing red. Instead, I grit my teeth and raised my hand.

A burst of red magic lit up the room, barreling straight towards me. I moved out of the way with a growl, barking out a spell that could change reality.

The lights in the house turned on, the room starting to spin as I was faced with none other than Hazard and two demons.

Hazard growled, sending another blast of magic towards me.

I fought the urge to laugh.

This witch was strong, but he wasn't stronger than me.

This time I reached out, grabbing the magic he had sent

towards me. I felt the rage in it, the desire to hurt. The desire to kill. I pulled it through the palm of my hand, letting it burn through my blood and bones before changing the energy to something different.

Protection.

The two demons at his side lunged for me, trying to corner me into the kitchen. I pulled on the energy of the spell, turning the floor into water.

Both of them fell through, their confused faces giving me a moment of satisfaction.

One of them snarled, shadow tentacles reaching for me. I jumped up onto the kitchen counter, hopping down on the other side.

The bedroom door flew open and Anne made a face of shock, but I flicked my hand, slamming it back shut.

I could do this alone.

Alex, I swear to the gods, if you don't open this fucking door, I will hang you by your balls.

Hazard and I slammed into each other, the two of us rolling over the couch and crashing into the coffee table. The wood cracked as I pinned him beneath me, overpowering his magic with mine.

His body went stiff, his face contorted with rage.

"You bastard," Hazard growled.

"Me?" I scoffed. "What the hell did I ever do to you Hazard?"

"You let him win," Hazard whispered. "You let him come back. And all of us who had finally moved on were dragged back into YOUR WAR!"

I sat back, shocked by his words.

The bedroom door flew open and Anne and Sylvia ran out, both ready to fight. I could feel Anne seething, but we'd talk later.

"There are two demons in the kitchen," I said, waving away the spell that altered the room. "They should be trapped in the floor."

I stood up, leaving Hazard frozen on the table. I sighed, taking a seat on the couch.

"I didn't mean for any of this to happen," I said to him.

"It doesn't matter," Hazard said, finally relaxing. "I'm fucked up. I like hurting people now, because it was either get used to it or die. But still. I'm tired. I want out. I've betrayed friends, monsters, witches, humans. I thought he was dead and then we were called up."

"Why are you telling me?" I asked.

I let him turn his head and he did, looking straight at me. "I want out," he whispered. "He will kill me for that though."

"I could kill you," I said.

"You could," Hazard said, letting his head fall back on the table. "If you wanted to."

"I don't want to," I said with a shrug.

Sylvia and Anne came back to the living room, both of them glaring at Hazard.

He looked at them both, his eyes widening. "Hi Anne."

I'd forgotten they had worked together.

Anne only hissed. "Fuck you."

Hazard sighed. "That's fair."

"I don't feel pity for you," I said, standing up. "But, we will send him back to hell. In the meantime, the only way to set you free is to kill you. Or make everyone think you're dead."

"There's no reason to help him," Anne said.

"No, there's not," I said. "But, I'd rather him go."

Anne only glared, the snakes around her head hissing at me in unison.

Sylvia reached for her, her touch almost instantly calming her.

"Why did he send you?" Sylvia asked Hazard. "Alex is very obviously a stronger witch."

"A distraction," Hazard said. "A warning. Our goal was to try and bring you to him alive, even though we knew that couldn't happen."

"How did you get past my wards?" I asked, frowning.

"Alfred," Hazard said. "He knows you're here obviously. But he doesn't know you're in heat, so you have that going for you."

I glared at him for a moment and sighed. This was a mess.

I looked up at Anne and Sylvia, grimacing. "I don't know what to do."

"I thought you could do this alone," Anne said.

Her words were sharp, and with our bond, they hurt even more.

"I'm sorry," I whispered. "I didn't want either one of you hurt."

"Alex, I could have eaten those demons for breakfast," Sylvia said.

My stomach twisted and I swallowed hard.

It would take awhile for me to understand that I wasn't alone after all this time.

Still, it wasn't fair to them.

"So," I sighed, standing up. "I'm going to make it look like you died, and then the three of us are out of here. As for your demon friends, they are going to remember what I tell them."

"I'm going to get a bag together with our stuff," Anne said, turning to go to the bedroom. "With nest stuff too, Alex."

My throat tightened again. "Thank you."

Sylvia gave me one more look and then followed Anne.

Fuck, I had fucked up.

Hazard watched them go and then looked back at me. "Thank you," he said, his eyes wide.

"If I ever see you again, I will actually kill you," I whispered.

Hazard nodded. "Understood. You never will."

The fear in his eyes made me believe him.

"Alright," I said. "Let's make the bastard actually believe this."

CHAPTER SEVENTEEN

fear

ANNE

After we had fake-murdered someone in the middle of the night, Alex made a portal straight to Inferna's apartment and the three of us showed up on their doorstep.

Inferna opened the door wearing nothing but a silky black slip, her eyes glazed over with sleep and her temperament already prickly.

"Good morning," I said, wincing.

Inferna blinked a few times and then stepped to the side, bidding us into her apartment. I had worked with her long enough to know what her motions meant, and that a pot of coffee needed to be brewing right now.

"Sorry about this," Alex said to her, shutting the door behind him. "We've run into a problem."

"Oh, I'm sure," she said dryly. "You're still in heat, Alex. What happened to fucking until you break it?"

"Alfred sent Hazard and some demons to my house."

"Well," Inferna sighed. "Fucking hell."

Art and Calen were already in the kitchen making coffee. It felt weird to see my other boss shirtless and in boxers, but hey— at least they'd managed that before answering the door.

Sylvia's hand slipped into mine and I gave her a gentle squeeze. I wished we would have mated last night, craving for there to be a bond between us.

Still, I could feel echoes of her through Alex, and then there was the connection we already had. She gave me a soft smile, one that worried me just a bit.

I had been through some crazy shit at the office the last few months, but none of it had been like what she had gone through, and I worried that the demons coming back to haunt us would hurt her.

She looked up at me, raising a brow. "I'm fine," she murmured.

"Okay," I said, giving her hand one more squeeze before letting go.

"I'm assuming everyone wants coffee," Art called.

"Yes," we all answered.

Inferna went to the living room, Calen leaving the kitchen to curl up next to her on the couch as she took a seat.

Sylvia grabbed Alex's hand and dragged him to another seat before he could melt from his apparent anxiety of invading their home this early in the morning.

Art pulled down several mugs and I went to help, the two of us pouring coffee and bringing them all to the coffee table that sat in the center of the room.

Alex leaned forward, burying his face in his hands for a moment with a sigh. "I hate this. I hate him. I don't even know how he knew where I was, or how Hazard was able to break in."

"What happened to Hazard?" Calen asked.

"We made it look like he died," I said. "Alex decided to spare him. The demons lost their memories of what happened and were sent on their way too."

Inferna snatched a mug up, settling back against the cushion, Calen leaning against her side. Art took a seat next to him, his hand settling on his hip.

There was such an easiness between the three of them, one that I hoped Alex and Sylvia and I would gain too. Alex would have to learn how to trust us first.

Alex ran his fingers through his dark hair, looking up at me as I took another seat, my tail curling around it. I cradled a cup of coffee, still digesting everything that had happened.

I didn't like being woken up suddenly. I rarely slept, and when I actually did, to be yanked from it so quickly immediately put me on edge. If Sylvia wouldn't have been there to calm me down, things would have gone differently. Hazard would be literally dead, not fake dead, and those demons would have been back in hell.

I cradled a cup of coffee to me, thinking about Alfred. We had done our best to ensure we weren't being followed, but it was difficult to make sure that there weren't spies in other places.

"We tried to make sure we weren't followed—"

Inferna waved her hand, cutting Alex off. "Don't worry. I already told you that you're not in this alone."

Art held up his phone. "I'm already texting everyone."

"Thank you," Alex sighed, leaning back. "I'm ready for this to be done."

"We all are," Inferna said, taking a sip of her coffee. She narrowed her eyes on Alex for a moment, and then looked at me, then Sylvia. "Who would have thought," she chuckled.

I raised a brow but smiled. Her assessment of the three of us was warm.

"Well," Art said, leaning and setting down his phone. "We have reinforcements arriving. I don't think it would be good to go to the office at this point since he has made this move."

"I don't either," Alex said. "I'm concerned for everyone's safety."

"You should worry about yourself," Inferna said. "The rest of us will be okay. None of us is the one in heat still."

Alex winced and I felt a prick of desire.

Sylvia looked up at me, our gazes locking for a moment. There was no place now for the three of us to take care of his needs until Alfred was gone.

The sound of a text message rang through the room. Alex paused for a moment and then reached into his pocket and pulled his phone out. I could feel the panic through the bond and already knew that the bastard had messaged him again.

"What did he say?" Inferna asked, reading him too.

Alex was frozen for a moment, his eyes flashing despite his expression being emotionless. "Has anyone heard from Cinder, Mich, or Lora yet?"

We all looked at Art. He shook his head, already hitting Cinder's contact to call. He hit the speaker phone, the ring echoing through the room.

My heart started to pound a little harder, anxiety working through me.

It kept ringing...and ringing.

Alex stood up, his muscles tense. "He says that he has

taken them hostage. All three of them. And that if I don't meet him alone, he will kill them."

His words chilled me to the bone.

"You're not going alone," Sylvia whispered.

"He isn't playing anymore," Alex said. "At this point, I should just go to him and handle him alone."

"No," I said, rising from my seat. "That's not happening."

"Anne— I can't keep—"

"You can't keep doing things alone," I hissed.

I put my cup of coffee down before I sent it flying. I then placed my hands on my hips, not afraid to challenge him.

"I'm doing this," he said, his tone darkening.

"Sure, but not alone," I said. "Everyone in here agrees."

"At the end of the day, it's my final say," he snapped.

We stared at each other for a moment, my temper becoming more and more volatile. "You're not my boss right now," I said.

"I still am—"

"No. Not if you do this. I will fucking quit and show up there anyway. You're not going to force us into doing what you want. We need to think more about this. How the fuck am I supposed to be able to rely on you as my mate when you obviously don't think you can rely on me? Or Sylvia."

Sylvia made a little noise and then stood too, crossing all of her arms. Alex looked at her, and then me, his brows drawing together.

I knew he didn't like being cornered or told what to do, but this was getting ridiculous.

"Also, how fucking dare you pull the boss card right now," I snapped.

Inferna, Art, and Calen sipped their coffee, watching the three of us go back and forth silently.

Alex took a deep breath, looking up at the ceiling for a moment to collect himself. I could feel the storm raging inside of him, and knew he could feel the one brewing in me. In Sylvia.

"No one has survived any of this by doing it alone," I said.

"True," Inferna echoed. "I think I have a plan, if you'd like to take a seat instead of being a jackass."

"We need to go now to make sure they're okay," Alex said.

"Well, first, I need to get dressed. Art and Calen too. Then we will make sure Cinder, Mich, and Lora aren't still home and that Alfred isn't lying. We'll give the three of you a couple minutes alone."

I watched as the three of them got up and went to a bedroom at the end of the hall, the door slamming shut.

The tension between the three of us was thick enough to cut with a knife. Sylvia was the one to break it first, touching Alex's shoulder with one of her hands.

He almost immediately relaxed, releasing a deep breath.

"I'm scared," he whispered.

I went to the two of them, looking up at him. Sylvia's hand slid into mine, giving me a soft squeeze.

"Alex," I whispered. "I have known you for months. I have been working with you for months. I have been through several dire situations with you where lives have been at stake. Where people have been hurt. I have seen you lie and be vague and be an ass. I've seen all of these things, but I still accepted this relationship because I believe in the good that is in you. I believe that we don't have to be alone anymore."

He swallowed hard, his cheeks flushing for a moment. Sylvia gave my hand another squeeze, her breath hitching.

"I haven't known you for long yet," she said. "But I know how it feels to think you have to be the one to do everything, but turning yourself into a martyr will make everyone lose except him. We love you, Alex. Let us help."

Alex was silent for a moment and then both of his arms circled us, pulling us close. Even though I was still a little angry, I still found myself pressing my face against his chest and Basking in the warmth of him. Breathing in his scent, the one that comforted me.

"I'm sorry," he said. "I'm stubborn. And I have my faults. I'm scared right now and I don't want to lose anyone else. Cinder, Mich, and Lora could be in danger right now because of me, and the thought of them being hurt makes me feel so many different things."

"We're going to save them," I said. "We're going to save them and put an end to this. It's going to be okay."

Alex nodded and kissed the top of my forehead and then Sylvia's.

We'd make it to the fucking weekend, even if it was the last thing I saw through.

CHAPTER EIGHTEEN
out of office

SYLVIA

W E HAD A PLAN. IT WAS A BAD PLAN, A RISKY ONE, BUT a plan nonetheless.

Ember, Lea, and Minni had checked the house for Cinder, Mich, and Lora— and it was true. The three of them were gone. There had been signs of fighting, and Cinder had left a sign for Ember that was one they had made in case there was danger.

Ember stood next to me, the two of us watching the entrance to the building from across the street.

"It's going to be okay," I whispered.

"We're going to have to play rock paper scissors over who gets to murder Alfred first," she said, glaring.

We were the lookouts, watching for anyone who went into the building. All of the lights were off aside from our floor, which was eerie to see. Cars passed us, the city coming to life as the sun started to rise.

My stomach felt sick. There was so much fear and anxiety, all of the emotions churning together. But, we had to be strong.

Ember held the walkie talkie to her lips as the person we were waiting to spot showed up on the sidewalk, heading straight for the doors.

Alfred's assistant.

She had a RBF that was hard to forget, and I knew it too damn well after being imprisoned too long. She had been one of the 'agents' to check on me regularly, making sure I was still alive. She was cruel.

We all doubted that Alfred cared about her, but kidnapping her could still be used as leverage.

"Go for agent bitch face," Ember said into the walkie.

"Ten-four," Billy growled back.

Billy, Jaehan, and Charlie had showed up ready to fight. Hell, all of us had.

This was the last time we would deal with this fucker.

I watched, knowing that I couldn't see Charlie as he moved through the crowd. No one could see him, which was something he had discovered he could now do at will. Turning his invisibility off and on took concentration, but he seemed to be enjoying it. I didn't know a lot about the three of them, but I was thankful someone was able to do that.

Alfred's assistant made it the door, only for her to suddenly freeze. Her hand struck out as she attempted to use her magic, but she was promptly pulled down the sidewalk and to an alley near the garbage cans.

"Let's go," Ember whispered.

The two of us left our spot, Ember waving her hand to use her magic to shield us from any spying eyes above.

We ran across the street, heading towards the alley.

Billy appeared next to us, the three of us going to where the assistant was now pinned down by Charlie's tentacles.

She let out muffled noises and growls, her eyes burning with fury.

"Good morning," Ember said, glaring at her. "Where is my sibling?"

Charlie let go of her mouth, which she opened to let out a scream until Billy casually held a knife to her throat.

"Listen," Billy said. "I really don't want to start my Thursday morning with fresh blood on my hands, but I will. We're not playing games and I remember you, you bitch. Answer the god damned question."

"The moment Alfred hears that Alex didn't come alone, they're dead," she hissed.

"Do you think Alfred would care if we killed you?" Billy asked. "Or are you like his little office toy? His lonely follower?"

"Shut up," she sneered. "Alfred is doing great things. He has a vision of the future."

"No, he has a vision for himself," Billy snapped.

"I'm going to ask again," Ember said, glaring. "Where are they?"

"I'm not telling you," she hissed. "I'd rather die."

Billy made a little tsk, shaking his head. "So be it then."

He started to move the knife, but then she let out a squeak, making him pause.

"Oh, so maybe you don't want to die?" Billy asked. "Or would you like it to be a little slower?"

"You fucking beast," she growled, glaring at him.

Billy snorted. "As if you haven't killed monsters and witches alike."

She was silent, her eyes still angry. "Fuck you."

"No thanks, I have my mates for that," he chuckled. "Answer Ember's question and we will let you go."

She stared at him for a moment and then let out a hiss. "Cinder is in Art's office."

"And Mich and Lora?"

"I don't know," she said.

Billy dug the blade in, drawing a bit of blood.

"I don't know!" she hissed. "I really don't! Alfred put them away, I just handled Cinder since they're a witch. Now let me go like you said."

Billy stared at her for a moment and then snorted, pulling the blade away. In one swift motion, he hit her hard enough in the head to knock her out.

Charlie's tentacles pulled away, leaving her on the ground.

"Well," I said. "That was...something."

"We'll focus on getting them," Ember said. "And then the other team will focus on Alfred."

I nodded and then leaned down, using my silk to bind the assistant. Within a few moments, she was thoroughly tied up and going nowhere.

"Your webs are handy," Charlie said, giving me a smile.

I grinned back at him, shrugging. "Sometimes."

"Alright," Billy said, putting the knife back in his jeans. "I'm ready for another three day weekend. I know Alex is your mate, so I mean this nicely, but I like it when he decides to pay us extra for no reason other than because Inferna tells him to."

I couldn't help but laugh. I had heard about the infamous three day weekends at Warts and Claws. Every time something bad happened, everyone got the following Monday off paid.

Our group looked up at the building, the rising sun

turning the sky golden. Steam rose from the ground, drifting up.

The walkie went off, Art's voice echoing. "We're in the building. Good luck, stay sharp, be safe."

The four of us looked at each other, nerves working through us.

We had all split up into groups, based on what made sense. Unfortunately it meant some of us weren't with our mates, but it worked for the best.

The four of us worked well together, and Ember was a powerful witch. Calen, Jaehan, Anne, and Lea were a team. The other was Minni, Inferna, Art, and Alex. Team A, B, and C.

Now that we knew C was in the building, the four of us could go on. They would be working towards Alfred, we would be working towards Cinder, Mich, and Lora— while the other team was working on taking out the henchmen.

We went to a door that was on the side of the building and Billy yanked it off the hinges. Charlie snorted, a little smirk resting on his lips that was almost idiotic adoration.

We were met with the cool air of the office building, and the scent of magic. The kind that burned, the kind that sent a shiver up your spine.

"Well," Billy muttered. "This is going to be fun."

All of us were ready to fight, our senses on edge as we moved down the hall. The lights flickered ahead, Ember and Billy staying in front while Charlie and I took the back.

"We're taking the stairs," Ember said.

We moved down the hall until we came to another set of doors where the steps started.

"Fuck, I really didn't plan for leg day today," Billy sighed.

"Shush," Ember snickered.

We all looked up the stair case as the doors clicked behind us.

It was ominously silent, every breath and sound that we made echoing like it was into a microphone.

"I don't like this," Billy muttered.

Ember sighed, pulling her purple locks back into a high bun. "Let's go."

The four of us started up the steps. Meanwhile, my monster started to rear its head, getting hungrier and hungrier to break truly free.

If I allowed that, I could take the three of us up much quicker. Ember was avoiding using too much magic to draw attention, but...

We hit the third flight and paused, Billy doubling over for a moment. "Fuck. You'd think being a top was enough of a workout."

"*Billy,*" Charlie hissed.

Ember and I both snorted, the tension breaking for just a moment.

"I could take us up easily," I said, "but I'd have to be fully shifted."

"Is there some danger to that?" Billy asked.

There was some, but mostly for those who might try to hurt me.

"It can be a little bit, but not for the three of you."

"Let's do it," Ember said. "Or else we're all going to roll into this fight covered in sweat."

The three of them took a step back, giving me room.

"More," I said, wincing.

They all took another step back and I turned, gauging the space.

Then, I finally let her free.

My body began to change, growing and morphing.

Bones and muscles snapped, my vision changing. Letting my most monstrous part free was always easy, it was chaining it back that hurt sometimes.

Within a few moments, I was fully shifted into a massive black spider. My legs felt the vibration of the building, my senses amplifying.

There were enemies above us, waiting for us to come up.

I could feel their intentions, their hatred.

"We're not alone," I whispered, my voice a feathery sound now.

"Didn't think so," Charlie said. "How...how are you taking us up?"

"Silk," I said.

I moved quickly, wrapping my silken strands around each of them. Two of my legs held on to the strands.

"I'm confused on how this is going to work," Billy said.

"We're going to guard her ass," Ember said.

I snorted, but she was right.

"I don't like this," Charlie said. He would have paled, but that was impossible for him.

I leapt up, my legs attaching to the wall. All three of them let out little squeals, but I was already moving rapidly.

We went up higher and higher, passing the staircases and landings easily.

We passed one of the landings, and I saw a dark figure emerge from the corner of two of my eyes. Ember let out a shout, and I felt her blast magic towards it, guarding our group.

Voices shouted above, confusion raining over our enemies as I took us past them in a blur. They were left confused and or passed out as Ember continued to send blasts of magic towards them.

We made it to the ninth floor and I stopped, cutting the silk loose. Ember, Billy, and Charlie hit the landing, rolling to their feet ready to keep fighting.

I could hear footsteps thundering as a couple other creatures came from above.

"Where the fuck is B team?" Billy growled. "I thought all these bastards were supposed to be out."

"I'm sure they're handling other stuff," Charlie quipped.

I gave in to the primal tide, allowing that part of me to take over even more. An orc and a witch hit our landing, but with three shots of my webs, the two of them were slammed into the guard rail and then sent tumbling over the other side.

Ember, Charlie, and Billy all turned to look at me with wide eyes.

"Can't ever trust the quiet ones," Billy mumbled. "I should have known that."

Ember made a face and then went to the door, kicking it open. The three of them went into the office, and I squeezed through the doorway, slamming it shut behind us.

The office was...

Silent.

It felt like a library, a forbidden one. One that we should not have been allowed in.

"I... don't like this," Billy whispered.

I didn't either. I stared down the hallway, my hearts pounding.

I could feel my bond to Alex tighten for a moment, his concerns coming through. Now, more than anything, I wished I had one with Anne too, but I had to trust that she was okay.

I closed all of my eyes for a moment, taking a breath. We had to trust each other. That was the hardest part about everything, but...

We would find Cinder, Mich, and Lora. We would take out Alfred, and then everything would be okay.

The four of us crept down the hallway, me following behind the three of them as I took up the entire space now. The lights continued to flicker, and now...now I heard a heartbeat.

"*Close*," I whispered.

The three of them nodded, all of our attention on high alert.

Art's office was not far now, just around the corner and on the other side of the floor.

Billy peeked around the corner and let out a hiss, looking back at us.

"I can see them," he whispered. "Cinder. They're tied up right in the doorway. There are two witches there."

Ember glared, her anger rising. "I can take care of them."

"*I can help*," I said.

The four of us looked at each other, a silent agreement being made.

It was time to fight— claws, webs, magic, and tentacles combined.

CHAPTER NINETEEN
take the bait

ALEX

I made it to the tenth floor fairly easily, which did not sit well with me.

I stepped out onto the floor, the one that belonged to me and Inferna, alone.

I was to be the bait— Inferna, Art, and Minni hiding and waiting for the signal. They were in the ceiling vents, having crawled around like spies.

The moment I opened my office, the air snapped with electricity.

Alfred was sitting at my desk, feet propped up and eyes already trained on me.

I met his gaze, not feeling a shred of fear.

No.

This meeting would be one from hell, but it was long overdue.

You're not alone, I reminded myself.

Alfred's nostrils flared, his eyes burning as he caught my

scent. I could see the hunger, the rage, the moment of confusion.

"You're mated," he said.

I closed the door behind me, going to the chair across from him and taking a seat. "I am," I said, my voice cold.

His teeth bared for a moment, a low growl leaving him. "The things I have done for you. All for you. And you dare sit here across from me, in heat but mated."

"I was never yours, Alfred," I said. "I never will be. You just refuse to accept the truth."

Alfred snarled, his feet coming off the desk and hands slamming down. He leaned forward, his mouth shimmering with heat.

"Hundreds of years together and you act like I'm the monster!" he thundered.

I stayed seated, watching him. I wasn't going to show him fear or give him the reaction that he wanted.

It had been a long time since I had sat in the same room with him.

It had been even longer since the two of us had spoken truthfully.

When was the last time I had told him no? Told him that he was wrong? I'd let him get away with so much.

It all would stop now.

"Alfred, you are the monster. All of the things you have done to people, and for what? All for me? I never asked you to do these things. The power has gone to your head. You're corrupt."

"This is exactly what you wanted," he sneered. "Monsters and witches to be closer, for monsters to have magic and witches be more beastly. You got exactly what you set out to do when you summoned me. You're just too weak to see it through."

"I've never been weak," I said, narrowing my eyes. "I summoned you. A powerful demon. Well, you were powerful. You were a lot more charming then too, and less of a fucking asshole."

"I haven't changed," Alfred said, shaking his head. "No. No, I'm just seeing what I should have done long ago."

"And what's that?" I asked, feeling the tension rise.

"Take your magic," he said. "And be done with you."

I glared at him, ready to spring into a fight.

"You didn't come alone," he said. "There's also that, which will need to be handled. I knew that you wouldn't. You'd rather let all of the monsters and witches die for you than be a bigger person and come alone."

That was what had fucked me up for so long.

Those types of words. Those types of beliefs.

Anne and Sylvia had finally shaken me to my core—reminding me that no, I wasn't alone.

No, I didn't have to be here alone.

I had to trust them to be able to do what they were able to.

I had to believe them when they said that they would be okay.

I had been taking so much power, hungry for it for so long. Driving myself to the brink of madness to attain it, all at the expense of myself. I had been lonely. I had been a bad leader. A bad manager.

A bad friend.

A bad person.

"They will have to be punished too," Alfred said. "They will have to die."

His words snapped me out of my thoughts and I rose to my feet. I could feel his magic, the stolen bits that belonged to omega witches. He shouldn't have had magic in the first place.

I would take it from him, once and for all. I would take it from him and return him back to hell, to a place he would never return from.

Alfred raised his hand, his claws gleaming in the ugly office lighting like razors. I raised my hand too, my magic buzzing at my fingertips.

Crack...crack...

I blinked. Alfred scowled and looked up at the ceiling.

Crack.

The ceiling suddenly gave way— the tiles collapsing, the boards and dust going everywhere as Art, Inferna, and Minni fell straight onto our enemy.

I watched in awe as they all hit the floor, a ball of bad words and chaos.

"For fuck's sake!" Inferna growled.

Alfred let out a string of curses as the three of them rolled off him, giving me the moment I needed.

I dove forward, using every ounce of my magic to restrain him.

Art rolled to his feet, immediately joining me.

Alfred let out a frustrated roar, only for Inferna to pop him hard in the jaw. The sound of his bones cracking had me distracted for a moment, even in the chaos making a mental note to never actually piss her off.

Minni kicked Alfred hard with a snarl, sending him down to his knees.

My magic burned through me, the air shimmering with blue heat. I felt the electricity run through me, the power rising up like a wave.

Alfred was frozen in place now, fighting against me. His

magic was much stronger than before, and holding him still was harder than I had planned on.

Sweat broke out across my forehead, the feeling of doom sending an icy chill down my spine.

Alfred's gaze met mine, his words a sneer. "If I'm going down, this whole place is going with me."

I felt his magic snap, cracking my own spell that was binding him for just a moment. His hand raised, revealing a button that was in his hands.

He pressed it before I could get him back under control. My magic snapped, keeping him from moving again, but it was too late.

All four of us looked up at the sound of an explosion.

Followed by another.

"Oh fuck," Minni whispered, her eyes widening.

The building groaned around us.

"You fucking bastard," I breathed, my rage finally tipping me over the edge. "Get everyone out," I said, looking around. "Now. I will handle him."

Inferna, Art, and Minni stared at me for a moment—but the sound of another explosion had them moving fast. Art was already drawing a portal, his eyes glistening with a hint of fear for everyone who was now in danger.

"We'll get them out," Inferna said, her eyes burning with fury. "We'll get everyone out before the building comes down. I expect to see you after."

"You will," I said.

She nodded and then went through Art's portal. The three of them disappeared, leaving me alone with Alfred.

He couldn't move but his gaze was still one of satisfaction.

Of victory.

"You haven't won," I said, the spell I had him bound

with becoming more and more volatile. "You will never win. They will get everyone out."

"They can try," he said as another explosion went off.

I felt my bond to Sylvia and Anne tighten, and that was it.

I didn't have time for this fucker.

This was the end of him.

I raised my hand, letting all of my magic flow straight into him. He snarled, his body struggling as I began to open a circle straight to hell.

"No!" he growled. "You need me! You need me to save them!"

"No, I don't," I growled.

He barked out a laugh as I poured more power until he realized that I truly was powerful enough to send him back.

"No," he said again. "You were meant to be with me!"

"I never was, Alfred," I growled.

The air howled around us as I opened a portal, heat flowing into the room. Alfred let out a harsh yell as his body began to burn, his soul being torn in half by me.

I could feel the magic exhausting itself faster and faster, but I didn't stop.

With a clean tear, his body burst into flames, his soul severed. Lightning burst from my fingertips and I sent him straight into the portal, letting everything go.

The lights went out, the floor grumbling beneath me as the portal shut.

Alfred was gone this time.

Gone and not coming back.

It would take a very long time for his soul to come back together.

He would not make it back here.

The only light in the office now was from the particles

of magic floating around me like embers and the morning light coming in from the windows.

The building groaned beneath me, a reminder that I needed to get out.

The floor started to crack beneath me.

Fuck.

I drew a portal through the air, one that would take me to the place we'd all agreed to meet.

I could only hope that I wouldn't be alone.

CHAPTER TWENTY
warts & claws

ANNE

The world was crumbling around us, literally.

I moved across the floor, dragging two monsters with me to the portal that Art had made. All of our teams had met back up only to split up again to get everyone out that we could.

We'd managed to find Mich and Cinder, but not Lora yet.

I could feel my bond to Alex, could feel the magic tugging harder. I was scared for him, scared that Alfred had hurt him. I was scared that something would happen to all of us.

We had all been through hell and back together, and I was thankful to know that if we made it to tomorrow— it would be the last time we would hear about the demon that was so desperate for omega magic.

I tossed the two monsters through the portal even

though they were my enemies. Even though these fuckers had tried to kill us.

The building started to groan again, threatening to come down.

"Fuck," I growled, looking back. "Lora has to be here somewhere. I'm going to go after her."

Sylvia brought a witch and a monster to the portal, pushing them through.

"We can't find her," Sylvia said, wincing. "We tried. We found Cinder and Mich, but I can't sense her even in my full form."

"We can't leave her," I said.

"We're running out of time," Art said, his eyes widening as part of the ceiling in the hall fell. "This entire building is going to go."

"We can't leave her," I said again.

Art let out a loud breath and nodded, closing the portal. "We have maybe five minutes. I don't know how to track her."

Sylvia made a face, looking at me. "I don't know either."

"She's part demon," I said, looking around. "Maybe a summoning circle?"

"I would need something of hers—"

The air shimmered next to Art, and Cinder came through with Ember, the two of them covered in dirt and blood.

"Cinder!" I hissed. "You're supposed to be resting."

"We have to find her," they said. "Mich is thankfully passed out or else he would be raising hell in here too."

"I can track her," Ember said. "But all of you should get out. Cinder and I will find her."

"No," I said. "I'm helping. But Sylvia and Art, both of you go."

Sylvia shook her head. "I can't leave you."

"Yes, you can," I growled, giving Art a look. "Go."

Art winced and opened up another portal, looking at Sylvia expectantly.

Sylvia let out a breath and then leaned forward, stealing a kiss from me. A warm one, one that was filled with love and yearning.

"Come back to me," she said. "In one piece."

I nodded, taking a deep breath. "Make sure our mate is alive," I said.

"I will," she said.

I then watched as she and Art went through the portal.

Ember grimaced. "Minni and Lea were mad I was going back in, but they were still helping the others."

I nodded and turned, the three of us now moving down the hall and going around the wreckage.

"I can feel her," Cinder said, taking the lead.

We went to the stairwell, following them. My heart pounded, my senses heightened as we all moved as a unit. The building groaned more, and I knew that soon, it would be coming down completely. Ember and Cinder would get us out before we were harmed, but Lora...

Cinder stopped on the sixth floor, pushing on the doors. They wouldn't budge.

All three of us immediately tried to push, but it was blocked.

"Stand back," Ember said.

Cinder and I took a step back, watching as she raised her hands and then sent a burst of magic that broke a hole straight through the wall.

I raised a brow, but we were on the move again, slipping onto the floor.

Cinder let out a breath, rushing down the hall to a door and kicking it in.

"There you are," they breathed. "My love."

Ember and I looked at each other and then through the doorway, seeing Lora. She was tied up, tears streaming down her face. Cinder cut the binds and then lifted her, holding her in their arms.

Their embrace made my eyes water.

"Oh fuck," she gasped, her arms wrapping around them. "Fuck, I couldn't break free. Oh my gods."

"I know," Cinder said.

"Where's Mich?!"

"He's okay, he's safe," Cinder assured her. "We're okay. We're all okay and getting out of here."

"I'm never coming back here again," she said.

"You won't have to," Cinder said, turning to look at the two of us.

I drew in a sharp breath, swallowing hard. I was so glad she was alive.

Cinder stole a kiss from her, the two of them whispering things to each other for a moment.

Fuck. I needed my mates. Desperately. Splitting up earlier had been one of the hardest things I had ever done, even though it had been for the best.

Warts and Claws had been my home for awhile now, but like Lora— I never wanted to come back.

I never wanted to see this fucking building again, which was good, because it was coming down.

"Alright," Ember breathed a sigh of relief.

"Fuck this office," I said, looking around. "Fuck this whole building."

"Agreed," Cinder said, waving their hand to create a portal.

The building started to move, the floor starting to crack as it made a terrible noise. All four of us went through the portal right as the ceiling collapsed, the end of my tail the last thing to come through.

We landed on the sidewalk, the sound of screams and chattering surrounding us. My eyes widened as I looked up, realizing that we were still in front of the office building.

The air burned with magic, the kind of power that shouldn't have existed. I felt my bond to Alex pull sharply again, pain radiating through my body.

I immediately moved across the street, weaving through people that were getting out of the way.

"Anne!"

I looked up to see Sylvia standing next to our mate— our mate who was almost blinding.

I ran to them, fear running through me again.

"He's going to push the building through a portal," Sylvia said, her six eyes wide with fear.

"There's no way," I said, looking at him.

He was unaware of us, his magic burning hotter and hotter. Alex's eyes were completely iridescent, his skin glowing.

"Alex," I whispered.

"He can do it," Sylvia said, her hand slipping into mine. "He can. He has that much power. We both know this."

It was true, although this...this could be how he lost that power.

I drew in a breath, watching as the building began to slowly fall. Alex let out a groan, and I felt pain rush through me. Sylvia let out a soft squeak, her hands holding on to me.

I didn't like that he was in pain. I didn't like any of this, but I still watched in wonder as a portal began to open.

Ember suddenly ran up, followed by Jaehan, Art, and

Calen. The four of them surrounded him, and Sylvia and I stepped back— watching as the witches worked their spells.

The sky darkened for a moment, and then the ground opened up beneath the building. Alex let go of the entirety and we all watched as it crumpled straight into the depths of wherever that lead.

The portal snapped shut and Alex fell back, passing out straight into our arms.

All of us surrounded him, standing in front of what was now just an empty lot.

"Fuck," Inferna said, her eyes wide. "That was..."

"Insane," Art breathed.

"Weird," Billy chimed. "Also, I quit."

"Same," Cinder said. They were still holding Lora, but Mich was with them now, battered but okay.

We were all okay.

Alex let out a breath and I looked down at him. I could feel as the magic drained from him and it felt... strange.

Sylvia and I held him close, waiting for him to speak.

"Hi," he whispered.

"That was amazing," I said, swallowing back tears. "You saved everyone."

"I didn't," he said, his voice hoarse. "Not at all. I just kept the building from hurting more people."

"Well, let's get out of here before the humans close in," Inferna sighed. "I'm sure this will be on the news."

"Oh I'm sure," Alex snorted.

He sat up with a groan, and then Sylvia and I pulled him to standing.

He waved his hand in the air, but stopped, unable to even make a spark of magic.

"I've got you, boss," Art said.

"Can we go to my house?" Alex asked. "I can order food and we can make sure everyone is okay."

"Yes," Art said. "You... need to make sure you're okay too."

Alex waved his hand, ignoring him. Art made a portal, one that all of us went through.

We landed in Alex's backyard, now away from the craziness that had just happened.

Tears filled my eyes. Did this mean that it was finally over?

"*Anne. Sylvia.*"

I looked up, my head spinning as Alex pulled me and Sylvia into his arms. I let out a choked sob, the three of us holding on for dear life.

We weren't the only ones. Everyone had made it out, and everyone was hugging someone.

We'd made it out of the nightmare that had become Warts & Claws Inc.

CHAPTER TWENTY-ONE

pizza party

SYLVIA

All of us were in the living room, every chair in Alex's house now taken. There was chatter surrounding me, everyone talking about everything that had happened.

I was happy because I was sandwiched between Anne and Alex, and both of them had yet to let me go since we'd made it back.

"I have ordered a lot of pizza," Inferna said, raising her voice to get everyone's attention. "Like *a lot* of pizza."

"I'd say that's some corporate bullshit, but it's hard to say no to pizza," Billy sighed. Jaehan and Charlie both chuckled at him.

"Well," Inferna said, snorting. "The Warts & Claws office is...kind of done now, I suppose."

"Is it?" Lea asked.

Everyone looked at Alex and he sighed. "Well, we have a couple of options. In both scenarios though, I would like to be taking a step back."

Everyone frowned, and I was surprised that Inferna was the one to say something. Lea and Minni both cocked their heads, Ember happily in Lea's lap. Mich, Cinder, and Lora were silent, watching him intently. Jaehan, Charlie, and Billy also had their full attention on him, curious.

"Alex, we do like having you as our boss," Inferna said.

Alex raised a brow. "I think you are the better leader. And I'm not saying that all of you have to *dislike* me if I'm not the boss anymore, but personally I am done with being in control. I want to take a step back, and if anything, you can be my boss. I'd rather focus on the financial part of the company instead of being the leader of everything else. I have been doing this for a long time and...I want to focus on other things. Today was a hard day for all of us, and none of you had to help. I didn't know that I would lose most of my magic today either. Still, I am thankful for the way everything has turned out. Alfred is gone. We are all safe. And I can look you in the eye and tell you I would rather not be the boss anymore, Inferna."

Inferna took a deep breath, crossing her arms. Somehow, even covered in grime, soot, and blood— she was still a badass. Art and Calen both watched her with reverence as she let his words fall over all of us.

"I have made a lot of mistakes on my path to power," Alex said. "I've been around for a few hundred years chasing a dream that led me to nothing but destruction. If some goodness can come out of it, then I will be happy."

"There has been a lot of goodness that has come from it," Ember said. "Look around you, Alex. All of us have found our mates because we ended up working at the office. All of us were brought together because of the mistakes that were made. And Alfred was the one who went crazy, not you."

"It's true," Jaehan said. "I mean... all of us here have been hurt by him, and you've tried to help. I don't think we can really blame you. And if you want to blame yourself, well... then, I forgive you."

That brought a resounding agreement from everyone.

Alex swallowed hard, letting out a breath as he leaned forward. I could almost see a weight lift from his shoulders, his body relaxing. "Thank you," he said.

I rubbed his back, giving him a soft smile.

"So..." Inferna trailed off. "What are the options then?"

Alex cleared his throat, leaning back against the couch again. "Restart the company completely from the ground up, continue to create an app that helps monsters and witches, and leave behind the hell that has been Warts & Claws Inc. I would help fund everything, you would be the main boss. And that's assuming everyone still wants to work. The other option is after today, we all walk away and go elsewhere."

"I said that I quit, but I didn't mean like *that*," Billy said.

I laid my head on Alex's shoulder, knowing that this was harder on him than he was letting on.

"If we restarted, I would want to change a lot," Inferna said.

"I'd imagine so," Alex chuckled.

"I'd change *a lot*, actually."

"Good," Alex said.

Inferna smirked, relaxing. "Hmm. Well. What does everyone think?"

She looked around the room.

Anne surprised me by raising her hand first. "I will stay if it's a new place completely and is restructured. But otherwise, I am done. And I want a vacation with my two mates where I can forget about working in general for a couple weeks."

"I second that," Ember said.

"I third that," Jaehan chuckled.

"Does everyone agree to that?" Inferna asked.

I looked around the room.

Everyone did agree.

Inferna's eyes landed on me. "And what about you, Sylvia?"

"I'd like to start working somewhere," I said, earning a few chuckles. "But I'd like some time with my mates too."

Anne leaned over and kissed my cheek.

"Okay then. Well," Inferna said, sliding down onto the couch cushion between her mates. "I guess the next question is what are we calling this company."

Everyone was silent for a moment and then Mich leaned forward. "Would it be amiss to call it Omega Inc.?"

The room was silent for a moment and then Billy snorted. "Honestly, that's pretty fitting."

"Can't complain," Art chuckled.

Inferna smirked. "It does work considering everything, hmm." She looked down at Calen, and his cheeks turned pink.

"I think it sounds good," Lea said, grinning. "Although maybe something like Omegasync sounds more app-like."

Everyone made an 'ooh' sound.

"I like that," I said with a grin.

"Me too," Inferna said. "Well, Omegasync it is then."

"Omegasync Inc.," Billy snickered.

"Catchy," Anne laughed.

Alex let out a soft hum and I looked up at him. He wore a soft smile, a slightly sleepy one. I could feel the warmth coming from him, a comforting wave.

All of us were exhausted. This week had been a whirlwind, while also being the longest week of my life.

A knock at the door had us all turning. Charlie got up, going to the door and bringing the twenty boxes of pizza that were delivered inside with his tentacles like it was nothing.

My mouth immediately watered.

"Okay, well," Inferna said. "Pizza and then we can reconvene."

Everyone got up and Anne went to the kitchen to help Charlie, pulling down a stack of plates.

I looked up at Alex again and he looked down, winking at me. I caught the faint scent of his heat and let out a soft growl.

"Hey," he chuckled. "Not here. Not yet."

"Soon," I said, wrapping my arms around his waist.

He pressed his cheek to the top of my head, holding on to me as our mate helped the pizza chaos.

"I love you," I whispered.

"I love you too," he said, tipping my face up. "More than you know. I am very thankful for you and Anne, and that you were willing to give me a chance."

Anne came back to us, holding two plates with pizza. "Eat up, you too. I want sex after everyone leaves."

Alex immediately blushed and I heard Inferna bark out a laugh from the kitchen.

Well, if Omegasync happened, it would certainly be fun.

By the time we all finished pizza, talked some more, and then everyone left for their own homes— it was well into the afternoon. Inferna, Art, and Calen were the last ones to leave.

"We'll talk Tuesday," Alex said, giving her a hug. "Thank you for everything."

"Thank you," she said. "Thank you for using your magic on the building. Many more would have been hurt."

Alex nodded, and we watched as the three of them left.

"Well," Anne said. "I think a movie, a nap, and some cuddles are in store."

"After a hot bath," I said.

"After I kiss both of you," Alex said, pulling us both to him.

I let out a soft moan as he pulled me into a kiss, my body melting against him. He then kissed Anne, and even she let out a happy sigh.

"Gods," I said, letting out a yawn. "My first week at the office was definitely something I won't forget."

Both of them laughed and I smiled to myself, happy that we were all off for a four day weekend, and able to put Warts and Claws behind us.

CHAPTER TWENTY-TWO
friday

ALEX

"Thank god it's Friday," Anne said with a groan.

The three of us were in bed, all a little battered and bruised but ultimately safe. Last night, we'd bathed, fucked, and then slept like the dead, waking up a lot happier now that everything was over. My entire world had been turned upside-down and had changed, but it was for the better.

I had to give up a good portion of my magic, but it was worth it.

Alfred was gone.

That's what I kept telling myself.

Sylvia curled up next to me, her arms wrapping around my torso. I let out a little chuckle, stroking her silky black hair.

"I think I could stay in bed all weekend," Sylvia sighed happily.

"Me too. Especially with both of you here," I said, smiling to myself.

Anne nodded, letting out a soft hum as her fingertips ran down my body to my cock.

I immediately let out a soft grunt, all of my blood rushing straight down.

"How do you feel about watching me finally mate with Sylvia?" she whispered, her hand gripping my now hard cock.

Fuck, I couldn't even think straight now.

Sylvia lifted her head, her eyes gleaming with lust. "Well, now I'm awake."

"I'd like that," I said, groaning as she continued to stroke my cock.

"To think you're still even a little in heat," Anne teased.

I couldn't deny that, although I wasn't sure I'd ever fully be out of it with Anne and Sylvia around. There would never be a day so long as I lived that I wouldn't want to be with both of them.

"I want you both to mate," I said with a deep growl.

Anne smirked, letting go of my cock. I swallowed hard as I watched her lean over, her hand sliding behind Sylvia's head and drawing her into a slow kiss.

Fuck, I was going to end up cumming just from watching them kiss.

I let out a heated breath, sliding my hand down to my cock and stroking myself as they both groaned.

"I've been wanting this so badly," Sylvia gasped as Anne kissed down her neck.

"Good girl," Anne purred.

"Fuck," I whispered, stroking my cock harder.

Anne groaned, pushing Sylvia back onto the mattress and spreading her legs. Sylvia gasped, which made me gasp too. I could feel the pleasure between the two of them, the lust and desire.

Sylvia arched her back as Anne flicked her tongue over her clit and then kissed her way up her body. Anne fit her hips between Sylvia's thighs, rubbing her pussy against hers as their lips met again.

"I can't wait to bite you," Anne breathed. "To mate you and make you cum. Get you ready for our mate. I want him to bury his cock inside of you."

"Please," Sylvia moaned. "Please. I need you too."

"Need," Anne teased, smirking. "So needy, isn't she Alex?"

"She is," I breathed. "Mate her, Anne. She's desperate for you."

Anne let out a soft growl and leaned forward, swiping her tongue over the red marking on Sylvia's chest. She licked her way up to her neck, her fangs gleaming in the morning light.

Sylvia's eyes widened, her gaze locking with mine as Anne buried her fangs into her neck.

Sylvia cried out, and so did I. I could feel it through my bonds with both of them, the electric connection of pleasure and lust. Of need and want and love. All of the things that the three of us had been wanting for so long, all answered in each other.

"Mate her," I commanded Sylvia.

Anne gave a nod and Sylvia didn't hesitate, sinking her own fangs into our mate.

Fuck. Pleasure burst through me and I stroked my cock, my orgasm crashing into me. I cried out, my cum shooting from my cock and dripping down. My hips jerked, my breath hitching as I gave every last drop.

The three of us were fully mated now, tied together forever. I pulled my hand away from my cock, letting out a soft groan.

Anne and Sylvia pulled their fangs free, licking the wounds that they'd just made. I watched as the mating bites almost immediately healed, leaving the silver markings of what had just happened.

Anne turned, immediately leaning down to clean up my cum. Sylvia did too, and my cock immediately hardened all over again.

"Fuck," I growled, feeling my heat rise all over again.

I had done my best to hide it while we had to deal with Alfred and the office, but now... now, I was free and I could completely cave to it.

"Suck my cock," I gasped.

Sylvia took the head of my cock between her lips, her tongue swirling over he tip while Anne worked her way down to my balls. I gasped as her tongue pulled one of them into her mouth, giving them a gentle suck.

"*Gods*," I cursed, the pleasure incomparable. "I love you both and— ah!"

I cried out, all of my words melting away as they both did a thing with their tongue that nearly sent me over the edge again.

Anne pulled back with a satisfied hum. "Ride his cock, mate. He needs to fill you with his next load."

Sylvia moved up, straddling me. She rose up, placing my cock against her opening.

I groaned, feeling how wet she was. She was practically dripping, her cunt begging to be filled with my cock.

"Take me," I grunted.

"Yes, Daddy," she whimpered, slowly taking my cock.

The hot heat of her pussy gripped me and I gripped the blankets, letting out a long moan as she took every inch. Anne then moved her body so that her hips were hovering above my face, allowing me to bury my tongue inside of her while she played with Sylvia's clit.

The three of us were intertwined in pleasure. I leaned up, immediately spreading Anne's pussy and licking her. I growled as Sylvia began to ride my cock, every part of my body engulfed in wave after wave of pleasure and lust.

The taste of Anne was perfect, the feel of Sylvia too. Sylvia let out a sharp cry, her voice echoing through the room as Anne continued to worship her body while she took me so well.

I was so close to cumming, and knew that the two of them were too.

"I'm going to cum," Sylvia gasped. "Oh please Daddy! Please fill me!"

Her beg was enough. I drove my tongue into Anne and felt her start to cum right as my cock jerked, another orgasm overtaking me. Sylvia's cunt squeezed me as she came too, the three of us succumbing to our passion together.

Anne fell to the side with a moan, melting into the blankets while Sylvia leaned forward, resting against my chest.

"Every day," I whispered, my head spinning. "I get to be with the two of you every day."

Sylvia smiled even though she was still in the haze after cumming, pressing her face against me. "I love you both. I feel so lucky to have you as my mates."

"I do too," Anne whispered. "A dream. A witch and a monster just for me."

I smiled, feeling very much the same.

"I'm lucky. And I love you both," I said. "More than I thought possible."

I had made a lot of mistakes over the years, but maybe everyone had been right yesterday. Maybe Warts & Claws had brought good things too...

I mean, hell. It had brought me to Anne and Sylvia.

I closed my eyes with a smile on my face, able to finally allow myself to feel the happiness of finding the two soulmates I'd spend the rest of my life with.

friday - two months later

ALEX- THE HEAD of Horny Resources

I SAT BACK IN MY CHAIR, LOOKING AROUND HAPPILY AT my office. I could hear the chattering of everyone else as we all worked, and was happy with my much smaller suite.

It had been two months since the end of Warts & Claws Inc. Omegasync was still in its startup phase, and everyone was happy.

Ember had become one hell of a team lead. Cinder and I worked closely together, able to be proper HR support and to bring on and train new hires. Minni and Lea had yet to join, but they liked to drop by unannounced and bring lunch as a treat for the thirteen of us.

Calen, Charlie, Jaehan, Billy, Sylvia, Mich, and Lora all made up a badass team of individuals who were able to do what they wanted— which was to help other creatures. Anne was still a wonderful secretary, and much more relaxed now that a demon wasn't breathing down our necks.

Then there was Art. He was a great boss. He was able to finally sink into his strengths and to work on other things, finding a rhythm that worked best for him.

Then there was Inferna, a great leader to all of us. Fearless, smart, sassy, fun, and incredibly kind.

Stepping down had been the best decision I had ever made for myself. I finally felt... happy with my life. Sylvia, Anne, and I had finally bought a new house with the perfect amount of space for the three of us— and were getting ready for a trip to the beach in a couple of weeks.

When I had started Warts & Claws, I had wanted to create the type of environment I got to work in now. I had wanted work-life balance, good benefits and pay, and to provide everyone with HR support who actually cared.

I was finally able to see that through.

The only thing that we had kept from Warts & Claws was the relationships— and the Horny Resources title.

Everything else had been built from the ground up.

A knock at the door drew my attention and I immediately smiled as Sylvia stepped in, beaming. "Hello good sir," she teased.

"Oh, hello ma'am," I said, grinning.

She came around my desk, immediately turning my chair so that she could straddle me.

"Hey, you two," Anne's voice interrupted.

We both looked up and I raised a brow, keeping Sylvia in my lap.

Anne smirked. "I think that's an HR violation."

"I think it is too," I said.

They both giggled and then Anne moved inside, slamming the door shut behind her.

Oh, there was that too.

There was an open door policy and a closed door policy at our little company.

Closed door policy meant that you turned around and walked the other way.

The walk of shame here was a lot more fun.

"I have some work for you," Anne said, coming around the desk and sitting up on the top.

"Oh yeah?"

"We both do," Sylvia said. "Some very hard work for you."

I grinned at both of them and raised a brow. "Well, let's get to it then."

With that, the three of us had a very productive meeting, and ended our workweek with a bang.

The End

clio's creatures

Hello Creatures 😍

My name is Clio Evans and I am so excited to introduce myself to you! I'm a lover of all things that go bump in the night 🌙, fancy peens 🍆, coffee ☕, and chocolate 😆

IF you had the chance to be matched with a monster- what kind would you choose?!

Let me know by joining me on FB and Instagram. I'm a sucker for werewolves to this day 🐺👻

P.S.

Join my Newsletter by clicking here- I won't spam you, but I will offer you fun rewards for being one of my monster loving creatures.

Clio's Creature Newsletter

thank you

Thank you to everyone for reading this series! I had a lot of fun with it, and have loved writing these characters.

To Erica Cooke— for being my amazing editor. Thank you for being a wonderful friend and for your support on this monster filled adventure.

also by clio evans

Creature Cafe Series

Little Slice of Hell

Little Sip of Sin

Little Lick of Lust

Little Shock of Hate

Little Piece of Sass

Little Song of Pain

Little Taste of Need

Little Risk of Fall

Little Wings of Fate

Little Souls of Fire

Little Kiss of Snow: A Creature Cafe Christmas Anthology

Warts & Claws Inc. Series

Not So Kind Regards

Not So Best Wishes

Not So Thanks in Advance

Not So Yours Truly

Not So Much Appreciated

Freaks of Nature Duet

Doves & Demons

Demons & Doves (coming Fall 2023)

Three Fates Mafia Series

Thieves & Monsters

Killers & Monsters

Villains & Monsters

Queens & Monsters

Heroes & Monsters

Made in the USA
Las Vegas, NV
30 December 2023